HOLDING HALEY

THE WEST SERIES

JILL SANDERS

GRAYTON

To my sisters . . .

SUMMARY

Haley has waited her whole life for Wes. They were secret sweethearts all throughout school until he shocks her by joining the military right after graduation. Heartbroken, Haley must wait until the day he comes home. But it's been five long years, and she has finally decided to move on with her life. That is, until he walks back into town, sexier than ever.

Wes has had one thing on his mind since leaving town —getting back to Haley. His experiences overseas have made him realize what he almost let slip through his fingers. All he wants now is to prove to her that waiting for him was the right choice.

*H*aley West sat on the edge of the pond and cried until she couldn't cry anymore. She was fourteen years old and now both of her parents were gone.

Her father's funeral had taken place just last week. It was still hard to believe that he wasn't there to talk to or go riding with anymore. Haley's mother had died when she was just four years old, too young to really remember her. But her first real memory was that of the shock, knowing that it was all because of her that her mother had been taken away from them. She grew up believing that it was her, and not the tornado, that had tragically ended their young mother's life, and she did everything in her power to make sure she never caused harm to anyone or anything again.

Feeling a nudge on her shoulder, she looked up at Dash, her gray quarter horse. He was the fastest horse on the ranch and he was all hers. Her pa had purchased him for her fourteenth birthday a few months ago. She had mentioned to him that she wanted to try her hand at barrel racing like her big sister, Alexis. After getting the new horse, she had tried it a few times but decided she liked running through the fields with him a lot more. They were so fast together. The horse seemed to know what she was feeling and thinking. He always took her to where she wanted to be, even today.

"I know," she told the horse. It was time for supper and she'd be missed if they didn't get back to the house.

Lauren, her oldest sister, was in charge of everything now, including her two younger sisters. Using the back of her sleeve to wipe her tears away, Haley started to get up from the soft ground where she'd thrown herself for a good bout of crying. She stopped when she heard a branch break not far from her.

All around the watering pond, the bushes and trees here were tall. Even this early in spring, the green leaves were very thick. It took a while, but finally she noticed a tall boy standing right beside one of the low branches of a large oak, just a few yards away.

"Hey," she said easily. She'd been born and raised in Fairplay, Texas and knew almost everyone who lived there.

"Hey," he said, stepping forward slowly. He was wearing an old blue and white shirt, his sleeves rolled up to his elbows. His jeans and boots were covered in dry dust and dirt, most likely from going through the fields. His dark hair was long and spiked up a little, like he'd run his hands through it. He had the darkest eyes she'd ever seen, but when he smiled, they lightened to a warm honey brown.

He walked over to her now and pulled her into his

arms. "I'm sorry," he whispered next to her ear. "We just got back in town yesterday from spring break at my aunt's in Dallas, and I heard what happened to your dad."

She nodded her head against his shoulder. She thought she'd cried all her tears out, until Wes Tanner held her close. She cried some more against his shirt. And when she was done crying, she finally felt like everything was going to be okay.

Haley was going to kill him. Her eyes bore holes into his back as he talked to his friends across the room. How dare he do this to her! Her arms were crossed over her chest. She tried to deny it, but she started to feel the sadness sinking in.

He hadn't even had the balls to tell her the big news himself. Instead, she'd had to overhear it from his best friends, who were talking a little too loudly at the party after drinking a few too many beers. But if what they were saying was true, she was going to kill Wesley Tanner and bury him where no one would find his ruggedly good-looking body.

She circled around the room for a few minutes, trying to calm herself down before she approached him. It was their graduation party and every senior in their small school was there, partying it up. Everyone was in a chatty mood, so it took her a while to make her way across the room.

When she was approached by Hannah, one of her

friends since grade school, she sighed, knowing she was going to be delayed yet again.

"Did you hear?" Her friend took her arm and pulled her towards a darkened corner. "Is it true?"

"What?" Haley felt like rubbing her forehead. She was sure she was slowly getting a migraine, but since she'd never had one before in her life, she couldn't be sure.

"Did Wes join the army?" Hannah asked, looking concerned.

Haley didn't know what to say. Should she tell her friend that her best friend and boyfriend since grade school had decided not to share this news with her? It was too much for her to think about. The betrayal was eating at her, so instead, she walked away, heading towards the door and some fresh air.

She walked out of the high school gym and headed towards the elementary school playground. Gathering up her long dress, she sat on the swing and removed her sandals. Pushing herself off from the sand, she started to slowly swing.

It couldn't be true. Her mind started running through all the scenarios of how she was being punked. Maybe Wes didn't even know what everyone was saying about him?

She was about to get up and go find him, to make sure, when she felt his hands on her back.

"Want a push?" he asked right next to her ear.

She quickly stood up and turned towards him. "Is it true?" she asked, crossing her arms over her chest.

He mimicked her stance. "Is what true?" He tilted his head and looked at her.

"Did you join the army? Are you leaving Fairplay for basic tomorrow?"

His eyes got big and his smile dropped away. "Haley, listen . . ." But she had turned and started walking away from him quickly. She didn't need to hear him say it. She saw the answer in his eyes; it was written on his face.

When he reached for her arm, she yanked it away.

"Why?" she shouted at him. "Why am I the last to know?" She didn't care if anyone heard them. He'd just ripped out her heart and tossed it aside.

"I meant to tell you . . ." He raised his hands to take her arms again, but she pulled away.

"Don't." She stepped back. "I've known you all my life. We've never kept anything from one another. Why this? Why now?"

"I didn't mean to. I've told you for a few years now that I was thinking about it."

"Thinking about it! Not doing it!" She shoved his chest, sending him back a step. His hands dropped to his side and she saw his head lower.

"I didn't think . . ."

"No! You didn't." She turned and started walking across the softball field.

She'd always imagined them getting married. They'd talked about it, but now . . . She turned and glared at him as he followed behind her a few steps.

"I'm sorry," he said, taking a step towards her. She let him reach out and take hold of her shoulders. The thin straps of her dress did little to prevent the chill that wracked through her as she thought about not seeing him every day. "I signed up last week and didn't have the courage to tell you. You know my father was in the army, and his father, and his . . ." He looked down at her and wiped a tear from her cheek. "I guess I didn't know what I wanted to do until last week, until . . ." He dropped off and looked at her.

She knew what he was talking about. Until the scare she'd had last week when she thought she was carrying his child. She looked down at her flat stomach and wished she had been pregnant. Maybe then he would have stayed. They could have gotten married and she'd have everything she'd ever dreamed of.

Turning away again, she closed her eyes and wrapped her hands around her arms tightly. "So that's it then? I've scared you away," she whispered.

"No." He came up behind her and pulled her close. "I guess it just made me realize that there's a whole world out there waiting for me." He sighed. "We're too young to think about starting a family." She felt him shake his head. "I just needed to do this." He turned her around again.

The lights from the school were too dim and too far away to see his face clearly, but she knew his dark eyes would be pleading with her. She was thankful she couldn't see the softness, so she didn't feel weak for caving, for caring too much.

Just then, Dale, one of Wes best friends, came running up to them. "There you guys are. Well, come on. We've got a going-away surprise for you." He grabbed Wes by the shoulders and tugged him towards the gym again.

She stood there in the dark field as she watched Wes walk away from her. Halfway back to the gym, he glanced over his shoulder at her, but she was sure it was too dark for him to see her sitting in the dirt, crying.

She drove home that night and refused to see him the

next morning when he knocked on her locked window. He banged for almost a half an hour before finally leaving. He'd slipped a note under the windowsill, but she didn't have the heart or the strength to read it. Instead, she shoved it in a large box with all her other memories of him. Then she carried it up to the attic where she locked it and her heart away . . . until he returned.

Six years later, Wes stood next to the softball field and smiled. It felt good to be home. Most of the town of Fairplay, Texas, was crowded into the large park area. Two different softball games were going at once. A women's team on one side and very young kids on the other. It was a wonderful contrast.

Families of every size and shape gathered around for the July Fourth festivities. He knew there would be lots of barbeque and watermelon, and after dark, fireworks. The noise level would grow deafening in the upcoming hour. It was a Fairplay tradition for as long as he could remember.

When his mother called to him, he walked across the sidewalk towards her. He felt like all eyes were on him as they noticed the slight limp he now had, but he smiled and held his head up high as he crossed over and kissed his mother's cheek.

"There you are. You would think that the army would have taught you to show up on time." She smiled and patted his cheek. "At least once in a while."

He chuckled. "I do like making an entrance." He nodded to the crowd. The softball game had actually stopped when his mother had called for him. He could see every eye on him, and almost every face had a smile on it, except for the pitcher in the game. And of course, she was the only one he'd been looking at.

For her part, she was looking at him like he was a ghost. When he waved at her, she blinked and dropped the ball. Fumbling, she bent down and picked it up, then turned her back to him.

The players on first and second base rushed to the pitching mound and talked with her for a while. A heated conversation followed, but Haley won out and turned back to pitch the ball. She took a moment to adjust, then threw one of the fastest balls he could remember seeing a girl throw, striking the batter out.

"That girl is the best pitcher this side of the Mississippi," his father said as he sat beside him. He had an arm full of Frito pies and Cokes. Reaching up, Wes took the food and passed some on to his mother as his dad sat next to him.

"She sure has an arm on her," Wes said, not mentioning that he knew for a fact that she had a lot of other great body parts as well.

She looked great. If he'd seen her earlier, as he was walking the short distance to join his mother, he probably would have tried to hide the limp a little better. He couldn't completely hide it, but he would have tried.

For the remainder of the game, she kept her eyes away from the stands. She played better than he remembered, and by the time her team had won, she looked worn out and frazzled. Her dark hair was a lot longer than the last time he'd seen her, and it was coming loose of the tight braid she wore. It was tied back with a blue bow like the other ladies on her team.

He could see the slight differences in her. Her hips were a little wider, her breasts were fuller—she looked good. She definitely filled out the blue and white uniform. Her skin was tan, and she had a nice glow going. She'd looked happy, like she was having fun—until she had seen him.

After the game, he stood around in the stands under the shade and talked to everyone. People approached his family, giving him handshakes or hugs and thanking him. He felt like a heel and wanted to be anywhere but there. Finally, after almost a dozen people had talked to him, he excused himself and started walking towards the dugout, hoping to find Haley.

She was there, surrounded by four of her closest friends and her sister Alexis. He didn't mind her friends, but Alex had a side of her that no one in town liked to cross. He'd heard that she'd married Grant Holton last year, and he hoped that maybe she had softened up a little.

"Wes Tanner, you have some nerve coming here," Alex said, crossing her arms over her chest like the other ladies were doing. Everyone except Haley, who was looking down at her feet like she wished she was anywhere but there.

"Lovely to see you, too, Mrs. Holton," he said slowly, then he smiled and walked over to her, giving her a light hug. "I'm glad to see you finally ditched Travis."

She frowned at him and nodded. "I guess you can say that the West sisters are not fools when it comes to finding the right man." She nodded and looked towards Haley, and he felt his heart sink. Was she trying to tell him that Haley was seeing someone? Or worse, married? He'd been so busy during the game watching her, that he hadn't asked his folks if she was involved.

When Alex and the other ladies noticed the shocked look on his face, they nodded politely to him and walked away, leaving him alone with her. Since she was still looking down at her shoes, he took that time to recover.

"Hey," he said when they were alone. She glanced up at him quickly, then bent to pick up her duffel bag without a word. He walked over and stood right behind her. "What was your sister talking about?" he asked after a moment of silence.

"I don't know what you're talking about," she said, stiffly. When she turned around, she bumped solidly into him. His hands came up to steady her. She tried to jerk away, but his hands held her tight. He missed touching her, being this close to her.

"Are you seeing someone?" he asked and watched her chin drop. Then as quickly as it opened, she shut it and jerked her shoulders back.

"I don't see how that is any of your business." She turned and tossed her bag over her shoulder, trying to block him out.

"It's not, I guess." He dropped his hands just as Tom Blake walked down the stairs.

"Hi." Tom nodded to Wes, then he watched the man walk up to Haley and plant a kiss on her cheek, sufficiently answering his question.

He felt his chest kick a little as he watched Tom take Haley's hand in his own. "You did wonderful out there," Tom said, trying to pull her closer, but Wes noticed when she hesitated. Just then, he knew he still had a chance with her.

He watched as the pair made their way across the field to where her family was. Her sister Lauren, brother-in-law Chase, and their new son were sitting with Alex and Grant in the shade of a row of oak trees. Their picnic table was full of food and it looked like they were staying for the fireworks that were due to start in a few hours.

His father walked up beside him, looking to where his attention was drawn. "Still have it bad for that girl, huh?" His father rested an arm on his shoulder.

"It never went away," he mumbled. His father chuckled.

"Don't wait too long. That Blake boy has been sniffing around her for a while. Sounds like they're starting to get serious." His father pulled him along to their picnic spot, where they had always sat. The old wood table was the same. He sat down in the spot where he had carved his and Haley's initials in the old wood. Playing his fingers over the worn letters, he looked over just in time to see her glance away from him. Smiling, he decided he just needed to come up with the right strategy. After all, love was the most important battle he'd ever fought, and he was determined to win this war.

CHAPTER 2

*H*aley sat back against the trunk of the tree and closed her eyes. The heat was getting to her. Even though she had changed into shorts and a tank top, she was still too hot.

She had hesitated when Tom tried to show affection in front of Wes. She was sure it was just Tom's way of staking his claim on her. But at this point, she didn't know if they were even really together.

It wasn't as if they were officially dating. They'd been friendly for the last year, but she had never really considered them a couple. They hadn't even really made out. Tom was shy. Too shy. She'd tried to push the relationship on, but every time she tried to get closer, he would back away. Just the other day she had convinced herself that it was time to move on. She had even talked to him and told him they were better off as friends, and he had agreed.

She opened her eyes and watched Tom with her family. He didn't fit in, not really. Everyone was polite to him, but there was something underneath it all. Almost like they were strangers to him, instead of family.

Glancing over towards Wes and his family, she realized he'd never had a problem fitting in with her sisters. They'd almost always treated him like their little brother, like he was part of the family. Even her father had treated him like the son he'd never had.

After seeing Wes, Tom started acting like they were joined at the hip. She'd had to persuade him that she had a headache in order to get some time alone, sitting under the tree. Tom was busy talking with her family, so she got up and started walking through the cool trees towards the small creek that lined the side of the softball fields. There was an old wood bridge that crossed the low water. She stopped and watched the turtles sitting on several large rocks, soaking up the sun.

She thought about all the times she and Wes had watched the turtles in the pond on her property. All the times they had lay in the tall grass or in the sand along the shore and kissed or made love. After he had left, she had missed him so much it had physically hurt.

But after the first year of not hearing from him, she had built up an immunity to the pain, a sort of callus over her emotions and heart. She had fully convinced herself that she would never feel that much again, as long as she lived. After seeing him again today, she knew she had been lying to herself all this time. It wasn't love she should have built up an immunity to, it was him.

"Hey." She jumped when he spoke behind her. She hadn't even heard him approach.

"Oh!" She spun around, her hand coming to her heart.

"Sorry," he mumbled. "I guess I'm used to walking

quietly now." He looked down at her hand over her heart, so she dropped it.

Not saying anything, she turned away, hoping to get her breath back. He was still so very handsome. When she'd seen him walking across the grass towards his mother earlier, she hadn't registered his limp at first. She'd only seen his face. His beautiful face. She'd always admired it. Even when it was a little pudgy in his youth, he'd always had the perfect chin, nose, and lips. Everything was perfectly proportioned on him. She had seen the subtle changes in him. He was full of rippling muscles that covered his arms, chest, and legs. He wore khaki shorts and a tight white T-shirt, which showed them off nicely.

He had always kept his hair a little longer. Now, however, it was military short, which reminded her of where he had been all this time and how he had kept himself away from her.

He walked up and leaned against the railing of the bridge. His foot rested on the lower rung. "I had hoped we could be friends."

She closed her eyes and sighed. She knew she was being ridiculous, but the hurt was still there, even six years later.

Turning to him, she looked into his brown eyes. Here, she noticed, he had changed, too. Gone was the softness of his youth. The naivety. His eyes were harder, surer somehow.

"I'm not sure." She turned and leaned back against the railing, looking more deeply into his eyes. She didn't even know what his plans were. Was he back to stay? Or was this just a family visit? A holiday?

She didn't see him moving until his arms were on

either side of her, resting on the railing. He was too close; she could smell him, and it brought back too many memories.

"Please." She started to push him away, but he reached up and grabbed her hands in one of his.

"Don't," he said softly. "Don't push me away again."

Her chin came up. "I'm not the one that did any pushing, if my memory serves me right."

"You pushed me away earlier. Listen, Haley, there is history here, between us. I just want to know if what we had is still here."

When he leaned in, she was too shocked to move. How was she allowing this to happen? Why couldn't she stop herself from wishing it would? She knew it would only take one word to make him stop. Why couldn't she just say, no?

When his lips touched hers, she sighed and felt her heart stir for the first time in years. How did he have this control over her? He moved closer and brushed his lips gently over hers again. It was like breathing for the first time in years. The soft feel of his lips against her own, the feel of his hands touching her, holding her. His chest pressed up against her own.

When he pulled back, there was a smile on his lips, reminding her of why this wasn't a good idea.

"No," she finally said, shaking her head quickly. "No, not again. Never again." She pushed away and rushed from the bridge. She heard him calling her name, but she didn't stop or turn back to look. She was stronger than this. She was strong enough not to walk into the storm. And that is just what Wes Tanner was, a raging storm ready to take away everything she'd been protecting for the last six years.

When she rushed from the trees, her family looked over at her with concern.

"What is it?" Alex rushed up.

Shaking her head, she took a deep breath. "Nothing. I . . . I have a headache and I'm going to head home." She walked over and picked up her bag.

"I'll drive you home." Tom walked over to her, but when his eyes darted behind her, she knew he had spotted the cause of her distress. Glancing over her shoulder, she watched Wes walk out of the trees, right where she had just come from. There was concern and satisfaction on his face. When he looked at her, he smiled slightly and nodded, then walked over to where his family sat.

The sun was just slipping behind the trees, and the field was quickly filling up with people who were spreading blankets and lawn chairs, so they could watch the fireworks.

"Oh, you can't leave now," Lauren said, pulling her close. "It's Ricky's first Fourth of July. He needs his aunts here." Lauren glanced over towards Wes. "Don't let him spoil our good time."

She sighed, knowing her sister was right. Besides, she didn't want Tom to drive her home and couldn't think of any excuse not to let him.

She looked over to where Wes stood looking at her and saw Savannah Douglas walk up to him and wrap her arms around his shoulders. Something inside her jumped when she saw the kiss Savannah placed on his lips. Although Wes didn't pull away, she could tell that he wasn't enjoying the attention Savannah was giving him.

Straightening her shoulders, she looked over at her sister and said, "You're right." Then she wrapped her arms around her sister. "I'll stay," she said, turning to the group.

Half an hour later, when the fireworks started, she wished she hadn't. Tom had laid out a blanket a little way away from her family. When he pulled her close, she sat up and tried to talk to him, but the fireworks were too loud, so she laid her head back against his arm and watched the show.

After the grand finale, she quickly sat up and asked that he take her home, knowing she would have the opportunity to talk to him then.

She sat in silence as Tom drove her back to Saddleback Ranch, the only place she had ever called home. The house had recently been remodeled by Chase, Lauren's husband. He'd moved in and fixed everything that had been going wrong with the place since their father's death.

Her sister still ran the ranch, along with Alex and Haley and a dozen or so hired hands each year. Their cattle grazed on over a thousand acres of rich Texas grass and were split and sold once a year. Each year, Haley picked the best calf and raised it to show in the county fair. It was her calling. She had a knack for picking out the best livestock. She loved helping to separate the herd, making sure to keep a handful of the best for breeding.

Ever since she was a child, her father had told her she had a way with animals. She just figured she had the patience and the extra love to really see what the animals wanted.

When Tom's car pulled into the long drive, he stopped behind her truck and shut off his engine. When she turned to him, he pulled her close and shocked her by placing a kiss on her lips. It wasn't as if kissing Tom was unpleasant, it was just that she had mentally made up her mind to break it off, officially. Pulling away, she tried to smile.

"Tom, I don't think this is going to work."

He sighed and shook his head. "No, I didn't think it would after . . ." He sighed again. "Not after knowing that Wes was back in town to stay."

Wes woke from the nightmare quickly. Every muscle in his body was tense. It took less than a second for him to realize he wasn't in the Middle East but in his childhood bedroom, in a bed that was almost a foot too small for him.

He took several deep breaths before his heart settled back in his chest. His vision was grayed, and when it finally cleared up, he could see the moonlight streaming through the blinds. He glanced over at the Batman alarm clock on his nightstand and sighed. It was one o'clock and he knew that was all the sleep he was getting for the night.

Sitting up, he ran his hands over his face. He wished that he wasn't in his parents' home, that he could easily walk down to the kitchen and grab a beer or some of those cookies his mother had made for dessert. But his mother was the lightest sleeper in town, and he knew that short of sneaking out his window, walking down the back patio, and pushing his car a few blocks before starting it, he wasn't going to get away with being awake at this time of night.

A smile crossed his face as he remembered all the times he'd done just that. Almost always he'd ended up at

Haley's, knocking lightly on her window until she came out and they would sneak away together.

Standing up and stretching his legs, he winced when pain shot up his left leg. Looking down at the nasty scar that ran from the middle of his thigh to just above his knee, he closed his eyes and sighed. He couldn't escape the last five years, in his dreams or physically.

When he walked to the bathroom, the old floorboards creaked under his feet. Tip-toeing the rest of the way, which he found particularly hard due to his leg, he decided that he needed to find a place of his own, and quick.

It wasn't as if his parents didn't want him here; he just needed to be free to come and go as he wished. At least without waking everyone in the house up while doing it.

Getting dressed, he decided he would take a walk. When he opened his window to crawl out, he felt the summer heat hit him and he smiled. He was used to the heat but had missed the moisture in the air that had been missing overseas.

He had always been thankful that his room was on the ground floor of the house. It made sneaking in and out easy. He knew his folks had known he was sneaking out, but as long as he hadn't gotten in any trouble and had kept his grades up, they hadn't minded too much. His father had always said that he didn't raise any fool. He had always taken that as a compliment since his folks had trusted him so much.

He started walking down his street. Most of the homes here looked the same. It was the middle of the night and dark as sin, but he could still see that the Regans left the TV running all night. Mr. Regan was probably fast asleep on his La-Z-Boy, where he'd slept for the last twenty-odd years; his wife had taken over his bedroom.

The next house was empty. He knew the McKormics were on vacation since their mobile home wasn't parked on the large drive they had built a long time ago. They traveled a lot since their two daughters had left home.

As he continued walking, he wished that he could drive up to Saddleback Ranch and Haley. What would she do if he knocked on her window now?

When he'd kissed her earlier that week, he had felt the old spark as before. But something had been missing. He knew he was to blame for her anger. It had only taken him two weeks in basic to realize that he'd been a coward. He should have told her he'd enlisted. There was no getting around the fact that he'd hurt her. Then to top it off, he'd made a point not to write or call her. After a year, he was sure that she'd moved on and thought it was for the best. She deserved someone who wanted to start a family and settle down, someone who would be there for her. And at that time, he just couldn't give her any of that because he was uncertain about his own future.

She'd been right when she'd accused him of being afraid, he'd been lying to himself. When she'd told him that she thought she was pregnant, he'd had a panic attack. Sure, he'd been excited, but a part of him was afraid, and in the end, fear had won. They'd been so careful, ever since that first night in her hayloft, when they'd been almost sixteen.

Up until their kiss a few days ago, he had thought that she was the only woman he could love. Now he knew that she was the only woman he wanted to love. He didn't have a plan yet, but he knew he had to think of one, and quickly.

Over the last few days, he'd asked around. It seemed that she and Tom had been seeing each other for almost seven months. No one in town thought they were serious since they had only been seen together on a few occasions. Before that, Haley hadn't seen anyone else, and that knowledge scared him. If she had been single all this time and had just started seeing Tom, she must be very interested in him.

He turned the corner and headed back to his house. His leg screamed at him with each step. He knew he had to go into Tyler to sign up for his therapy, but he'd been putting it off.

He desperately wished he could jog again, something he'd done his whole life. He'd placed first in the 1500 meter and 400-meter hurdles at regionals, not to mention the awards he'd gotten for the high jump and sprints.

Looking down at the way he walked now, he wondered how long it would take him just to get the pain to subside when he walked across the room. It had been almost three months since he'd been hurt, and he knew the emotional scars would be with him a lot longer than the physical ones. He'd lost several of his closest friends that day.

When he crawled back in his window, his body was too tired to continue thinking about everything he'd lost over the last couple years. Instead, as he lay down in his small bed, still fully clothed, his mind drifted to the past and he dreamed of making love to Haley in the loft on a cool fall night.

CHAPTER 3

"I don't care if it takes all day," Haley said, putting her hands on her hips. "I told you already that I'm taking him and that's final." She looked across the room at her sister and for the first time in her life wondered if she wasn't going to get her way.

Lauren sat at the table and stared at her. Ever since she'd become a mother, Lauren had learned how to push it until she got what she wanted. But Haley was even better at it.

Finally, after what seemed like a millennium, Lauren sighed and relaxed. "Fine, but you have to take your cell phone with you and call me the second you two get there."

Haley smiled and pulled out her fully charged the phone from her back pocket. "Yes, Mother." She giggled and walked over and kissed the toddler that was sleeping in her sister's arms. "It should only take me a few hours. I have everything packed, and I promise there won't be any trouble." She turned to walk out.

"Haley," Lauren said and waited until she stopped at

the door and looked back to finish. "Be careful. I used to think I was indestructible, too."

"I know." Haley smiled at her sister and walked out to greet Dash. He was older now and a million times more stubborn then when he was younger, but he was her favorite man in the entire world. Dash had never been mean to her, never left her, and had never broken her heart. She walked up to him and patted him on his silver mane.

"Are you ready to go have some fun?" she asked him as she made sure her pack was secure on the saddle. He nodded, a trick she'd taught him the first year she'd gotten him.

They took their time, winding through the hills on their way up to the old cabin site. The original cabin that her grandfather and father had built had been burned down last year by drug runners who had used their land and almost killed Lauren in the process. Chase had moved a smaller modular home up to the site.

The clearing was a little bigger now, but since the location played a big part in their cattle business, it was needed. Cattle roamed those hills during winter and spring; in the fall, they were herded back and separated for auction.

During the summer, the cabin stayed empty for the most part. Haley and her sisters had gone camping with their father up there until his death when Haley was fourteen. Even with the new mobile home, the place still reminded her of their father.

Dash was getting older, and therefore it took twice as long as before to make it up the hills. She had to stop several times along the way and let him rest, but she didn't mind. This was her time. Lauren had begged her to take Lauren's horse, Tanner, since he was faster and not so old, but she just couldn't make the trip without Dash. She knew this was probably the last trip she'd make up here with him and she wanted it to be special. She'd even packed a few extra apples in her pack for him.

Since he knew the trails so well, she had only to hold on and let him lead. Several times along the way, she had actually drifted so far off into her daydreams that she'd almost dropped the reins.

Her mind was consumed with Wes. Since seeing him last week, she'd been doing a lot of thinking and dreaming about him. Actually, it was because of him that she was heading to the cabin for the weekend. If there was one good thing about being alone with yourself for a few days, it was that there was plenty of time to sort out your thoughts on a subject.

At the house, there were too many distractions. Work, the animals, her sisters, and even little Ricky made it almost impossible to think. Normally, she would welcome all the hectic attention, but she had some serious soul searching to do and decisions to make.

Reaching the cabin just before dark, she pulled out her cell phone and called Lauren as she walked Dash into the new barn Chase had built.

"I'm here, safe and sound," she said as she pulled off her packs and started brushing Dash to get him ready for the night.

"Okay, umm . . ." Lauren said. Haley could hear Alex in the background, saying, "Tell her."

"Tell me what?" Haley asked only to hear silence on the other end.

"You got her into this, you tell her," Lauren said, and Haley could hear the phone being passed to someone else.

"Haley." Chase's voice came on the other end. "I didn't know you were heading to the cabin this weekend, and well . . ." He paused. "I ran into Wes at the Grocery Stop yesterday and he mentioned how he was looking for a place to stay and, well, I sorta told him he could stay there for a week until one of the ranch hand places opens up."

Haley dropped the phone and walked to the door of the small barn. Sure enough, she noticed there was a small light in the window. Looking over to where the new dirt road was, she saw his truck parked under the tree there. Closing her eyes, she wondered if the night could get any worse.

Turning back into the barn, she thought about loading up Dash again and heading down the mountain, but she was too responsible of a horse owner to take an old horse down the windy paths in the dark. She picked up her phone to Lauren's concerned voice.

"Yes, I'm here," she said, using her other hand to rub her temple. She didn't normally get headaches, but a massive one had started along her temple. "Any chance you can come to pick me up?" she asked, knowing the answer. It was almost a half hour drive up the dirt road, not to mention that she would have to leave Dash up here until tomorrow. "Never mind. There are two bedrooms. I'll just make do."

"I'm really sorry about this, Haley. Chase had mentioned it to me, but I was so tired from staying up with Ricky, I didn't think about it when we talked."

"It's okay. It's not like I'm going to murder him in my sleep." She chuckled and said goodbye to her sister.

Taking her time, she finished up in the barn and started walking towards the house. Wes stood on the small front deck, his arms crossed over his chest.

"Chase just called me." He smiled a little.

"Yeah, I figured he would." She hoisted her bag over her shoulder and stopped at the bottom of the steps. "We aren't going to have any problems, are we?" she asked after a moment of silence.

His eyebrows shot up. "Problems?"

She sighed. "Listen, Wes, what we had was great, but we were kids. It ended over five years ago. I think we both know that we can't just pick up where we left off."

He nodded, and for a moment, she thought that would be the end of the conversation.

"Of course," he said slowly. "But nothing is stopping us from starting something new."

Two hours later, as she lay in the small bed in one of the bedrooms, she couldn't stop playing his words over and over in her mind. "Nothing is stopping us from starting something new."

Of course, there was something stopping her from starting something new. History. She wasn't an idiot. He'd hurt her once. What was to stop him from doing it again? Did he honestly think that she would just willingly jump in bed with someone who had torn out her heart?

She'd been so frustrated after he'd made that statement outside that she had walked into the house without a word. After dropping her bag off in the empty room, she had marched into the small kitchen and cooked a can of soup she'd brought along. The entire time she sat at the small table and ate, he'd sat across from her and watched her.

She'd felt so agitated that every time he tried to start

up a conversation, she'd shut him down. Finally, after eating, she'd excused herself to shower and had locked herself in the room all to herself. So much for being alone to sort her thoughts.

It took a while for her to finally shut down, but the long day of horseback riding finally caught up with her and she drifted into a deep sleep. She was woken some-time later by moans and screams from the next room.

Rushing into to Wes's room, she saw him lying on the bed in just boxers. He was thrashing around with a night-mare. Her eyes roamed over his arms and chest, which were a lot wider than before. The new muscles looked great on him. Her eyes traveled down his chest to his stom-ach, past his boxers to a large puckered scar on his left thigh. Since it was dark, she couldn't see very clearly. When he started moaning, she rushed to his side and shook his bare shoulders until finally, his eyes flew open. His arms reached around her, pulling her down next to his half-naked body.

"I was having the worst dream," he said in a groggy voice as he buried his face in her hair, which had come loose from its braid. "There was this explosion . . ." His voice dropped off and she felt his body tense. Then his grip loosened around her. "Haley?" he asked. She could hear from his voice that he'd finally awoken.

"Yes," she whispered, not wanting to let him know how it affected her to be so close to him again.

"I'm sorry," he said after a moment, then he released her shoulders, so she could sit up and look down at him.

It was too dark to see clearly, but the soft moonlight that drifted in the windows was enough that she could see his bare chest against her palms. She had tried to push herself completely away from him but had stopped just short of moving off the bed.

"Are you okay?" she asked, looking down at him.

"Yeah," he said, rubbing his hands over his face. She could feel his newly gained muscle; it was so different from the last time she'd seen him and felt him like this. Her mouth went dry and her mind found a million things to focus on. How wide his chest looked, how big his pecs were now, how he'd kicked the blankets off; her eyes refused to focus on anything but his navel. Her eyes found the dark trail of hair down his stomach enticing, which only made her wish she could pull his boxers away, slowly.

When she heard Wes chuckle, her eyes flew to his face, and she realized that his brown eyes were laughing at her.

"What?" She pulled back further.

"I thought you were a dream." He sat up a little, and her eyes flew to his chest and arms again.

When his hand came to rest on her shoulder, she jolted out of the fantasy her mind had been playing.

"Come here," he whispered.

Her mind cleared for just a moment and she shook her head.

"Please." She heard his voice crack a little.

His hand was running over her naked shoulder. The tank top she'd worn to bed was large and had loose straps. Her left shoulder strap was down around her elbow. His rough hands felt so good next to her skin.

"I . . . I can't do this again." She pulled back then stood next to the bed, looking down at him. His eyes raked over her and for the first time, she realized she was wearing his old gym shorts, the ones he'd left in her room one night.

She'd been wearing them for as long as she could remember, and had thought nothing about it, until now.

"I'm sorry I woke you," he said, his eyes moving up her body until he reached her own eyes.

She nodded, not able to say anything. When he pushed the sheet aside, she released the breath she'd been holding. She realized that he was wearing a pair of army shorts, which hung loosely on his hips. He walked over to her. She backed up towards the wall until her back hit the door.

"Haley," he said, his hands going to either side of her shoulders, pinning her in place. "I meant what I said earlier. There's nothing holding us back from starting over."

She looked into his dark eyes and, for a moment, she was transported to another time and place.

"Do you trust me?" he asked her, walking closer to her. Wes had just turned sixteen, and she was still a month shy of her sweet sixteenth birthday. It was the middle of the night and he'd snuck out of his house again. This time, when they walked up to the hayloft in the barn, she knew they wouldn't stop at just touching each other. This time, they were going to make love.

She nodded her head and pulled him close. As they kissed, he backed her up until her knees had hit the soft hay. He laid out a blanket, so the hay wouldn't scratch her soft skin. He pulled them down until he rested next to her, then he took his time peeling her clothes from her, layer by layer until she was fully exposed next to him.

She didn't feel shy, not when he looked at her like she was a goddess. His dark eyes roamed over every inch. He stood and pulled off his own clothes, which she watched with great interest.

When he stood over her, completely naked, she felt her confidence waver for the first time. He was so big and she was still unsure what to do. Then he'd rushed to her side and kissed her again and nothing mattered except him.

When he touched her, she felt something almost too hard to explain. He was more than her soul mate. When he kissed her, every bone in her body had turned to mush. Her skin tingled and her heart beat out of her chest.

Then he was above her, sliding into her, stretching her until he made her his, completely.

"Well?" he asked, bringing her back to now. He was a breath away from her and the memory of him inside her, filling her completely was still fresh in her mind. But the hurt of the last five years outweighed the beauty of the past.

Shaking her head, she said, "I can't." She looked down at his chest, then closed her eyes to the beauty of him. "I can't expose myself to that kind of pain again." She straightened her shoulders and looked up into his eyes. "I won't."

His hands dropped to his sides, his eyes searching hers. Then he stepped back. "I understand." He turned and walked back to the bed, and she noticed how much he limped. Her eyes went to his legs, but his shorts and the dark made it impossible to see the damage again. She turned to go, her hand on the doorknob. "Haley?" She looked over her shoulder at him. "I mean for you to trust me again. Soon," he said to her back. She rushed from the room, her heart racing. She lay in bed and dreamed of their first time, in the hayloft, so many years ago.

❄

When Wes woke up, Haley and Dash were both gone. It had taken him almost three hours to get back to sleep after she'd woken him. The image of her ran through his mind over and over. How she looked, smelled, and even felt, had caused him great pain as he lay there looking up at the ceiling. Knowing she was just in the bedroom next to him hadn't made it any easier.

He knew he had to come up with a plan to win her back, especially after seeing her last night. Having her this close only solidified that need even more. He had thought that staying out here, at Chase and Lauren's cabin, would be best for him. He could have space and time to decide his next move. Now he felt like he was just hiding from the choices he had to make, and from her.

Packing up his stuff, he made a call and was relieved when Chase informed him that one of the houses their ranch hands usually stayed in had come open sooner than he'd thought.

He knew there weren't a lot of empty places to stay in Fairplay. He'd been thinking of buying his own house, but right now, there were only ten places available on the market. He'd looked at all of them and had been seriously disappointed by almost all of them. Most of them were so run down that it would have been better to clear the lot with a bulldozer and build a new home. There were only two that had possibilities, and out of those, he'd really liked the one on Bond Drive up near the state forest. It was almost ten minutes out of town, but the lot was in good enough condition. He knew and liked the neighbors if you could call them that since their home was almost three miles down the state road.

He wanted to put an offer on the place but was waiting

for the VA to finish an appraisal and approve him for financing on a double-wide, which he planned on putting on the land somewhere. The process, he was told, would take a little over two months.

Driving into town, he pulled into Mama's just as his stomach growled.

The old place looked the same. There were new awnings outside and it looked like Mama had replaced the front windows recently. When he opened the door, the smells and sounds flooded his mind with memories.

Jamella, aka Mama, stood behind the counter, frowning at him. "Bout time," she said in a rich Louisianan voice, which boomed over the entire dining room. Every eye turned to him standing just inside the door. "Well, don't just stand dar." She walked around the counter and opened her arms. "Come give mama a hug." Her accent came out much stronger when she wanted it to, or when she wasn't paying any attention. He walked easily across the floor and into her arms.

Her laughter was quick and loud. "Bout time you got home." She pulled back and looked at him. "You got skinny, boy."

"No, ma'am, just taller." He smiled.

"Don't talk back, boy." She smiled. "Willard, make up a special plate. Our boy's back from fightin' for our freedom."

Willard, the cook who'd been working at Mama's since anyone could remember, poked his head out the opening and smiled.

"Good to see you, Wes."

Wes nodded as Willard disappeared again, and Jamella walked him over to an empty booth. "You stay right dar.

I'll bring you out a Coke and your food." She turned to go, but then turned and looked at him and sighed. "Sure, is good to have you back in one piece, boy."

Over the next hour, he was fed some of the best and greasiest food he'd had in a long time. Everyone who stopped in sat at his booth and talked to him. It was nice catching up with everyone and he'd heard all the latest gossip in town. He'd heard all about how the old Mayor's wife had gone plumb crazy two years ago and how Travis had hightailed it out of town. Even though the Mayor— well, ex-Mayor—was still living in his big house, he was half the man he used to be; no one in town blamed him. Or so he'd been told over and over again.

He heard how the new mayor, William Davis, was working hard to bring order to chaos after the big ordeal.

By the time he drove out to Saddleback Ranch, he was all caught up on what had happened around town since he'd left. His folks weren't the kind of people to gossip, and most people in town hadn't known he'd been injured or that he'd been honorably discharged from the army a few months ago. Apparently, his father and mother were the town's only introverts. There was a part of him that was thankful for the privacy. This way, he could tell the town a short version of what had happened, leaving out all the details and the guilt.

When he drove through the iron gates, he stopped his truck and smiled. The place looked good. The last time he was here, things hadn't been kept up so well. Now, however, there was a new green roof, and new windows and shutters, and it looked like the whole place had a fresh coat of paint.

He could see fat cattle grazing in the back fields, and

there were a couple men on horses working near the corrals to the side.

When he drove up, he realized one of them was Chase, and he waved.

Stepping out of the truck, Chase pulled a tan horse to a stop next to the truck.

"Evening," Chase said, taking his hat off his head and wiping his brow with a bandana.

"Looks like you could use a few more hands." Wes nodded to the corral, where they were trying to brand some cattle.

Chase laughed. "We could always use a few more hands. I have the keys to the place here. I moved a few things around, but it's yours, if you need it, until the end of next month." Chase tossed him down a set of keys.

"Thanks." He pocketed the keys. "I hope to know something from the VA in Tyler soon."

"Do you have a job lined up?" Chase asked, dismounting from the horse.

"A few possibilities. Actually, I was thinking about asking Stephen Miller about a job down at the station."

Chase smiled. "Wanna be a deputy?"

Wes nodded. "I was thinking about it. I studied law enforcement for two years before deploying."

Chase slapped him on the back. "Well, doesn't that beat all."

"But I'm dying to ride again, so if you need a hand around here . . ."

Chase laughed. "Anytime you want to lend a hand, just grab yourself a horse."

The heat was getting to her. She'd spent the last six hours on the horse and wished for just a moment out of the saddle. Not to mention a cold shower. Branding new calves was hot and sweaty work and usually lasted a whole week. It was a full-time job when you had acres and acres of them to do.

She looked over the corral full of little ones and their bellowing mamas. It always put a smile on her face to see how many they had and how healthy all of them were.

There were a dozen ranch hands at any given time working the fields, and she usually knew all of them by name. She liked most of them, at least the ones that came back year after year.

There were four ranch hand houses along the side of their property, which had been there since before she was born. Two of them had been rebuilt after the tornado that had claimed their mother's life had come through. Most of the workers stayed in their own travel trailers in the park area her father had built shortly after the tornado. They could hook up with water, sewage, and electricity and most of the men preferred it that way. Some of them even chose to live there year-round, rent-free as long as they worked.

All in all, she was very proud of what her family had built here. She whistled for Dingo, their family dog. The dog fancied herself a shepherd and always helped with the calf sorting. Not only was she a smart dog, she had more patience than any person—or dog for that matter—that Haley had ever known.

Dingo cut across the field and separated two calves from their mamas, leading them into the corral with a little help from Haley and Bobby, one of their quarter horses, which had been named by Alex.

"You make that look easy," someone said next to her. She almost fell off the horse when she heard his voice. Looking over, she saw Wes on top of Lou, another one of their quarter horses. They were going to have to stop letting Alexis name all their animals.

"What are you doing here?" She knew she sounded harsh, but this was her time. Her ranch. She didn't want him here now.

He smiled and tipped his hat. "Working off my rent." He pulled Lou closer to her horse.

"Don't—!" she warned, but it was too late. Lou leaned over and bit Bobby on the neck, causing the horse to jump and jolt. When she reached for the reins, she missed and went flying through the air. When she landed on her butt, her vision grayed with pain.

Then Wes was beside her, trying not to laugh. "Oh, my god! Are you alright?" He took her shoulders in his hands, trying to hold her still.

"Yes, fine," she said between clenched teeth. "Just

leave me alone." She tried to push him away, but he pulled her up onto her feet and proceeded to run his hands over her. "Stop!" She tried to push him away again, but he continued to look her over. Finally, she grabbed his hands and looked him in the eyes. "I'm fine, really."

She saw concern and laughter in his eyes. "I'm sorry."

Caving, she laughed, even though the pain was still predominantly in her mind. "It's okay. You didn't know that Lou doesn't like Bobby."

"Who? What?" He ran his hands down her braid.

"Lou." She nodded to his horse, which was grazing nearby. "Bobby." She nodded to her horse, which had run into the corral, as far away from Lou as possible. "They don't like each other. I suppose it all started with Cindy." She dropped his hands and started brushing the dust off her jeans.

"Cindy?" he asked, watching her.

"Yeah, they had a misunderstanding. Cindy is attracted to Bobby, and Lou is jealous because he liked Cindy."

Wes chuckled.

"What?" She looked up at him and frowned.

He laughed again. "It's just that you're talking about the horses like it's a soap opera."

She stopped dusting off her jeans and looked at him. She laughed. "I guess when Alex gives them human names, I start thinking of them as such."

When she stopped laughing, she looked up into his eyes.

"Are you okay?" he asked, his voice low as he stepped closer to her.

How had he gotten so close? Why was she letting him get this close? She was trapped in his dark eyes.

Today, in the light, they looked lighter. She could see the hazel freckles in his irises. His hand was running up and down her arms as he leaned closer to her. She felt herself leaning closer to him, drawn in by his eyes.

Just then, Chase broke in. "Is everything okay?"

She pushed back from Wes and looked up at her brother-in-law. "Yes, Lou got at Bobby, who tossed me off. Can you go grab him for me?"

He laughed and shook his head. "I guess we need to deal with that. I'll go grab him." He set off on his horse, toward the corral.

"Why are you here?" She turned on Wes once Chase was gone.

"I told you. I'm working off my rent. I moved into one of the ranch houses yesterday."

She felt the tension building. "You what?"

He laughed. "Don't look so upset. It's just until I find out about my loan."

She tensed. "Loan?"

He smiled. "I'm trying to buy a place."

"So, you are sticking around?"

He nodded. "I'm hoping to."

She looked off towards the corral as Chase rode towards them with Bobby following behind.

"Stop by my place tonight and I'll tell you all about it. I'm in the closest house to the road," he said just before Chase arrived. She didn't have time to answer before he was hopping on Lou's back and riding off to help the other men gather up the calves.

She couldn't stop watching him. The way he sat on the horse. How he held himself. He looked every bit the part of the cowboy, from the worn, tan Stetson he had on his head down to the dust on his battered boots.

He'd changed so much physically in the years he'd been gone. She sighed as she looked across the field at him, thinking about how it used to be, how it would be now. Then she cursed as the calf she'd been trying to herd escaped her for the third time in less than ten minutes.

"Are you even trying to get that little guy?" Alex asked, coming up behind her.

"What?" Haley looked over at her sister, an image of her and Wes popping into her mind.

"The calf there. Roger has been running you in circles for almost ten minutes." Her sister nodded to the little brown calf that looked like he was having a fun time letting her chase him around.

She chuckled. "Roger, huh? I suppose you'll want to keep that one, too."

Alex sighed and leaned on the saddle horn, looking around. "If it was up to me, I'd keep them all."

Haley smiled. She too had her favorites. She had a knack for picking out the blue-ribbon calf from the herd. Looking down at Roger, she thought he could easily fit that description by the end of the season.

"Fine, we'll keep Roger." She turned Bobby and started walking her horse next to Alex's.

"Great." Alex smiled. "Now, are you going to tell me what you plan on doing about Wes?"

Haley frowned. "No."

"Oh, come on." Alex reached over and stopped Bobby from walking with a tap. "You've always had your nose in Lauren's and my business, now it's our turn."

Haley smiled. "Yeah, but you two didn't know what

you had right in front of your faces." She looked over at Wes. "I know for a fact that what that man has, I no longer want. I can't afford to go there again."

"Haley." Alex waited until she turned and looked at her again. "We all make mistakes; we all can make choices that take us down the wrong path. Don't let something someone did years ago ruin what's meant to be."

Alex reached over and patted Haley's leg, then turned her horse towards the herd and got back to work.

Over the next hour, she thought about what Alex had said. Was she willing to chance it again with Wes?

She'd never told her sisters about the scare she and Wes had years ago. Maybe his reaction had been a male standard. Maybe she should forgive him for taking off like that. Could she trust him not to do it again? He said he was staying around— everyone in town was talking about it— but so far, he didn't have a job, a car, or even a permanent place to live.

By the time the sun was going down and everyone was calling it a night, she had come to a decision. She would wait and see if he was serious about sticking around. But she needed to protect herself.

After grabbing a cold shower and a ham sandwich, she headed out to the barn to check up on her animals.

As she walked out the back door, she smiled at the picture her sister and family made. Lauren, Chase, and their son Richard, whom everyone called Ricky, were on the back deck, swinging in the over-sized swing Chase had built for their last anniversary.

"Going to check up on the animals?" Chase called out to her.

She nodded and waved. When she turned the corner by

the barn, she bumped into a solid mass of muscle. Looking up, she groaned when she saw Wes smiling back at her.

"Evening," he said, slowly.

"What are you doing here?" She knew it came out a little whinier than she intended, but at this moment, she didn't care. He was invading her life.

Before she realized what, he was doing, his arms were around her and her mind went blank. She looked up to tell him to let her go, but when she saw the heat in his eyes, everything else disappeared. The world could have been on fire and she wouldn't have noticed.

Wes couldn't stop looking at Haley's face as he held her. He wanted to pull her closer, but she held herself so stiff that he knew she would pull away if he tried.

"You smell wonderful," he whispered.

She blinked a few times and he could see her green eyes focusing again. He'd always loved that he could see her emotions reflected in them. They were almost like mood rings, letting him know when to move in or when to back off. Now they were telling him to take a step back, so he dropped his arms and leaned away.

"Going for a walk?" he asked, knowing he was switching subjects before she could reprimand him for being at her place.

When he'd asked her to stop by his place, he'd known she wouldn't come. After sitting on his porch for half an hour, he'd started walking and had ended up here.

"Listen, Wes…" She looked over her shoulder, towards the house.

"Don't. Just take a walk with me. I haven't seen you in over five years." He knew he was pleading, but he wanted to spend time with her. Even if she couldn't stand him, he still wanted to just be with her.

She sighed and rolled her shoulders, a move he knew meant that she was doing some serious thinking.

"Fine, but only to the shed and back." She nodded to the light on the old watershed.

"Great." He took up her hand and started walking slowly. "So, my mother has told me a little of what's happened in town since I left. Maybe you can fill in gaps." He looked over at her and saw that he'd successfully confused her. She was expecting him to talk about them, but he wanted to keep her mind off the fact that he was going to win her back, slowly. He'd learned how to be stealthy the first year in the army. Sneaking in and catching the enemy was sometimes the only way to get what you wanted.

She sighed and dropped his hand. "Well, you heard all about Lauren and Chase?"

He nodded a little. "Mom told me that they'd been married the day after your father's funeral." She nodded, as he laughed. "Then just last year when he moved back, they fell in love. Not the usual order of doing things."

"Yes," Haley smiled. "They make such a wonderful couple. Now with Ricky, they are perfect." She looked off ahead and sighed again.

"And Alex and Grant. Tell me how that happened," he asked, humor lacing his voice.

Haley laughed and stopped to lean against the fence along the path. "No one seems to know, other than the fact that it was much needed. Grant came in at the right time, I guess." She smiled. "Of course, he's changed a lot from when he was a kid." She turned and looked at him and he noticed in the dim light that her cheeks turned a dark shade of pink.

"What?" he asked, leaning his foot on the bottom rung of the fence. He was close to her and could smell her sweet scent. How he'd missed that smell over the years.

"Nothing," she said, shaking her head. Then she turned away, leaning back against the fence. "Chase has worked so hard to fix the house up." She nodded towards the house.

There were lights that hung on the back deck, in the trees, and along the awnings, making it look very romantic. He could hear the crickets and frogs as they chirped their nightly ritual. There was no place on Earth that he wanted to be more than right there, with Haley.

"He's doing a fine job. He's started work on the place I'm staying in, too." He laughed. "Actually, that's why he's allowing me to stay there. I'm helping him out by painting the place next week."

Haley turned to him. "Chase is fixing up the ranch homes?" When he nodded, she continued. "You know, I'm always the last to find these things out." She looked a little upset, so he changed the subject.

"What about you? What have you been up to since I left?"

She turned back to him, looked him in the eyes, and shrugged her shoulders. "Same old stuff, I suppose."

"I hear you've had a winning calf the last three years in a row at the state fair," he said, playfully, reaching up to tuck a strand of her dark hair behind her shoulder. She'd always kept it long, but this was the longest he'd ever seen it.

She shrugged again. "Yes, and I think I found number four just today."

He smiled. "You have always had such a talent with animals." He pulled her closer until they were a breath apart.

"Wes, I can't do this." She swallowed and pushed away from him. "I understand why you left. I was just as scared as you were." She took a few steps away from him. "But you hurt me." He could see the hurt as her eyes pleaded with him. "Can you understand that I can't take that chance again? I've moved on." She started walking back towards the house and all the lights. "You should, too."

He watched her as she made her way to the house. She stopped on the back deck and talked with her family for a minute, then disappeared into the house. He stood there against the fence until he watched her bedroom light turn on, then a half an hour later, turn off.

As he made his way slowly towards the house that he was calling home for the next few weeks, he couldn't stop wondering what it would take for her to trust him again.

He'd never imagined how it had been for her, staying in Fairplay while he went off to basic and then overseas. He'd been too preoccupied with keeping himself alive to think of how she'd been alone in the small town.

He loved Fairplay, but there just wasn't a lot to see or do if you didn't have someone to share it with. Sure, she had her family, but now that both her sisters were happily married, maybe she was feeling some pressure to get hitched as well. Maybe that's why she was letting Tom stick around? That thought almost had him turning back around and knocking on her bedroom window. But he could already see the porch light of his little place and continued on.

When he finally lay down in bed, he stared at the ceiling for hours, thinking of how he could convince Haley to give him another chance. He knew one thing—moving slowly wasn't going to work anymore. He had to up the stakes and fast.

CHAPTER 5

The next few days, Haley stayed busy with work around the ranch. She didn't have a major role in how things ran around the pace, but she did all that she could. She enjoyed mucking out the stalls and feeding and watering the animals. But her favorite job was riding the fences, checking for breaks in the barbed wire.

Dash wasn't the fastest horse, but he knew the routes to take by heart, and he was smart enough that when he saw a hole for her to fix, he'd stop. Most of the ride she could let her mind wander; since she had a lot to think about, she hardly paid attention to the job.

When lunchtime rolled around, she parked the horse under a tree and leaned up against the large trunk. She ate a sandwich and a bag of chips and washed it all down with a bottled water. After eating, she fell asleep, lying in the cool shade. She jumped when she heard something.

"Sorry." Wes looked down at her, smiling. "I didn't mean to wake you."

She shook her head, trying to clear her foggy mind.

"No, you didn't. I was just resting my eyes." It was a lie since she still couldn't focus her eyes; she knew she must have been in a very deep slumber. She wanted to stand, but he surprised her by taking the spot next to her under the tree. His knee pressed up against hers, causing her heart to flutter.

"It's a great day for napping under an oak." He smiled again, and her heart jumped.

"I suppose." She turned her eyes away from his face and looked off to where Dash stood, eating some grass.

"How's the old boy doing?" She looked back at him in question, then he nodded towards her horse.

"Dash?" He's doing fine." She looked at her horse again, afraid of saying anything more.

"Haley," Wes said, taking her hand in his, "we can't keep on ignoring each other like this."

She sighed and looked at him again. His brown eyes pleaded with her. "I know, but we can't go back to the way things were, either."

He looked down at their joined hands, a sad look in his eyes. "I understand that." He raised his eyes slowly and heat spread throughout her body. "But there's nothing stopping us from starting all over. We're different people than we used to be. I want nothing more than to learn all about you again." His hand ran up her arm slowly, sending little goose bumps over her skin. "Explore what we could be." Her eyes were locked with his; she couldn't look away from him. "Maybe we can have something wonderful again." He leaned in closer until he was a breath away from her lips. "I'm game if you are." He waited, and when she blinked and looked at his lips, he moved in and gently laid his lips on hers.

She'd dreamed about this moment since he'd brushed her lips with his weeks ago. She'd imagined how it would feel to really kiss him, wondered what she'd do. None of it came close to the reality of his lips on hers, his hands on her soft skin.

Her fingers went into his hair, holding him close so she could further explore the way he felt now. His lips were like a perfect memory, but there was a hint of newness there as well. His hair was still cut military short. She explored his neck and shoulders as his hands ran slowly over her arms.

When he moved to lay her down in the soft grass, she jolted and pushed away. Shaking her head, she cleared her mind of the images she'd been playing over in her mind. She wasn't ready for this. It had been years, almost six to be exact since she'd been intimate with him; she wasn't ready to jump back in bed so quickly, not after being hurt so badly.

Wes must have guessed her thoughts. He sighed and rested his forehead on hers. "Someday. Soon."

She shook her head. "Wes," she started, but he placed another soft kiss on her lips to stop her.

Then he looked her in the eyes and repeated, "Soon."

As they rode back towards the house, she asked him questions about his travels. He was hesitant at first, but by the time they made it to the barn, he had opened up a little more and told her where he had been stationed and how long he'd been overseas. She knew a little about what he'd been doing over the years, as much as she could learn from his folks without sounding too desperate. But for the most part, no one in town knew what had happened to him, why he now had a limp and a sad look in his eyes.

"Come to my place for dinner," he asked as they cooled off the horses and brushed them down.

She shook her head. "I can't. I have plans tonight." She kept her eyes focused on her task and was surprised when his hands rested on her shoulders, turning her around.

"Haley…" His voice was rich and soft. "Are you and Tom an item?"

She laughed a little. "No, we were, but . . ." She shook her head. "I'm not ready for a relationship."

"Why?" He rubbed his hands over her shoulders.

"You." She was pinned between Dash and Wes and felt like there wasn't enough air in the large barn.

"I didn't mean . . ." He dropped his hands and stepped away. "I know I hurt you." He ran his hands through his hair, something that would have sent his dark locks standing straight up years ago; now, however, his short hair stayed perfectly in place. She missed seeing him frazzled like before.

Walking up behind him, she put her hand on his arm. "Wes, we've been through a lot together." He turned back to her.

"I'm sorry," he blurted out. "I'm sorry for not telling you about signing up for the army. I'm sorry for leaving you after . . . after . . ." He cupped her face. "I should have never abandoned you like that."

She didn't realize there were tears falling down her face until he gently wiped one away. How could she have known that his apology would mean so much to her? That after all the years she'd been waiting to hear those words, they would still mean so much. She'd tried for so long to understand why he'd left her. They'd been so much more than lovers; they'd been best friends.

"Why?" Her voice squeaked, and she tried to cover the emotions.

"Why?" He wiped another tear from her face.

"Why did you leave? Was it because of . . . the scare?"

He looked at her. "I suppose so. I guess I was scared that I wouldn't experience everything that was out there." He shrugged his shoulders and stepped back. "I didn't realize what I had." He walked to the end of the stall and leaned against the post, looking off towards the doorway. She could see he was uncomfortable with the conversation.

"You don't have to explain," she started, but he broke in.

"It's not that. It's just," he looked around again. "This isn't how I planned on talking to you." He motioned around to the stall. "Break your plans tonight, come to dinner. Give me a chance to explain."

She sighed and leaned back against Dash, then nodded.

His smile was instant. "I'll see you at seven?"

She nodded again.

After he left, she went up to the loft, one of her favorite thinking spots, and wondered what she'd just agreed to. She sat there for a few hours before she heard someone come into the barn and shake her out of her thoughts. Walking into the house, she realized she had just over an hour to get ready for dinner.

There were still so many questions in her mind. Was she willing to take another chance with Wes? Did he deserve it? Why couldn't she rid herself of his power?

She'd learned one thing in the last few years after seeing both of her sisters fall in love with great men— sometimes you just had to take a chance and hope every- thing worked out.

Deciding the best course of action was to make Wes suffer while she made up her mind, she took a little extra time picking out her outfit for dinner. She even went as far as applying some of the makeup and perfume that Alex had left in their joint bathroom.

By the time she started walking over to the ranch house, she was determined to make Wes work hard so she could get some answers.

Wes had a million things to do before Haley arrived at seven. First, he had to run into town to buy some food. Then he had to clean the entire place. Even though it was small, the construction had left the place looking like a tornado had gone through it.

He drove to the Grocery Stop with a list of items he needed. As he walked through the narrow aisles, Savannah walked over to him and grabbed his arm. He tried not to sigh in frustration.

Everyone in town knew Savannah was an attention seeker. And since he was getting a lot of attention around town for recently returning home, she had been hanging on him a lot.

"Well, isn't this a coincidence, running into you here." She ran her hands up and down his biceps. "And just look," she pointed to his cart, full of items from his list. "It looks like you're getting ready to have a dinner party. I sure hope I'm invited," she purred in his ear loudly enough for anyone else in the small store to hear.

"Hi, Savannah." He tried to move away from her, but

she had too tight of a grip on his arm. "No, just getting some basics for the place."

"Oh, well." She pouted a little. "I heard you're living out at Saddleback in one of the hired hand places. Surely, we can find you a better place to lay your head," she said, running her hand over his chest now. He got her invitation clearly but acted like he didn't.

"I enjoy staying out at there. I'm looking for a little solitude for a while. Well," he tried to move forward, but she was having none of it. Looking around, he found out why. There were a few people standing around, acting like they were grocery shopping, but really they were listening to their conversation.

"Well, the least I can do is bring you out one of my famous pecan pies tonight. After everything you've done for our country, someone should welcome you home properly."

He smiled. "There's no need. Besides, I have dinner plans. But"—he pulled her hands away from his arms— "I appreciate the offer." He quickly pushed his cart down the aisle and disappeared into the frozen food section.

He could hear people talking but didn't pay any attention as he continued his shopping. He stopped by the flower shop on the outskirts of town and bought the largest bouquet of flowers they had, keeping Haley's favorite colors and flowers in mind. The fact was, he knew everything there was to know about her, and yet he felt like he didn't know enough.

It took him a few hours to clean the house after putting the groceries away in the recently painted kitchen. After showering, he started dinner, a meal he'd learned to cook from one of his best friends before they'd been deployed to different countries.

Eric had been deployed to Tangier, Morocco, to help with relief after a mudslide hit a small town, killing hundreds. Wes, of course, had been deployed to the Middle East.

He was just finishing the final touches in the dining room when he heard the knock at the door. He couldn't explain why he felt nervous, but as he opened the door, his fingers shook.

Then he saw her and his breath was knocked out of him. She wore a long flowing tan skirt and a white lacy tank top. Her hair was loose, and she'd applied some make-up to her face, which highlighted her pink lips and green eyes. She looked beautiful.

"Are you going to let me in?" She chuckled nervously.

He realized then that he'd been standing inside his door for the past minute, just staring at her.

"Oh." He felt like banging his head against the door for his stupidity. "Sorry." He moved aside as she walked by. Then the smell of her perfume hit him and he felt his knees go weak.

She stopped just inside his living room. "I've never been in this one before." She looked around.

"Really?" He walked over to her. "I would have thought you would have been in all of these since you grew up less than a mile away, and they all belong to you." He smiled.

She shook her head. "My dad never wanted us to bother the men on 'their' time." She air quoted. "When Lauren took over, she wanted us to follow the rules. Of course, she's been in all of them to see if they needed any upkeep." She turned in a slow circle. "It's a lot nicer than I imagined."

"I can give you a tour if you want?"

She blushed a little and shook her head. "No, that's okay. Something smells wonderful."

He nodded and took her hand. "Food first. We still have a few minutes before it will be ready. Let's head outside."

The house was small, but it had a big deck off the back kitchen. He'd set the table, making sure to place a bunch of newly bought candles all over the railing and table. When they walked out, the place glowed with romantic light and soft music, which played from his iPhone speaker.

"This is nice," she said, walking to the railing. The stream that ran behind the row of houses added to the romantic feel. The frogs and crickets were chirping their nightly tunes.

She leaned on the railing and looked out across the field towards the lights of the main house.

Walking up beside her, he moved closer. He turned his back to the view, choosing to look at her face instead of the scenery.

"Yes, it's a lovely spot." He smiled when she looked up at him.

"Why are you staying here?" She turned and leaned on the railing, facing him.

"Because Chase and Lauren invited me to." It was simple enough to him, but he saw her frown a little at his statement.

"Why here? On my land?"

"You know why." He reached up and brushed a strand of hair away from her face. "You."

She shook her head, dislodging the hair again. When she tried to take a step back, he took hold of her shoulders. "Haley, I know what happened in the past, how I hurt you. I'm not the same man I used to be. You're not the same woman either." He pulled her closer until he felt her heart skip against his. Her hands had gone to his shoulders, but so far, she hadn't tried to push him away.

When he looked into her green eyes, he felt something return that he thought had been long gone. Leaning down, he placed a soft kiss on her lips. Meaning to go slow, he felt a jolt when her hands went to his hair and pulled him down for a passionate kiss. Her hands roamed down his neck to his shoulders and arms. He felt himself start to shake and wrapped his arms around her more tightly. Her tongue explored his mouth until he moaned and felt himself stir. When it became almost painful, he slowly pulled back and smiled down at her.

"I told you I would explain." He ran his hands over her soft shoulders. "Let's eat; I'm sure the food is ready." He watched her green eyes clear a little. She nodded and leaned against the railing again.

CHAPTER 6

*W*es had made one of her favorite dishes. The Greek chicken was so juicy and spicy, she found it hard to concentrate on anything but eating every bite. When her plate was empty, she leaned back and smiled at him.

"I've missed this." She nodded to her plate.

"I figured you'd like it." He smiled as he finished the last bite of his plate. "I didn't get to cook as much as I would have liked overseas."

"I tried making this once." She shook her head. "I failed miserably."

He laughed at her and she couldn't help but smile. She'd miss the sound of his laughter as well as his cooking.

She waited until he took another sip of his beer, knowing that his mood had changed, that he would attempt to explain why he'd done what he had years ago. Why he had, in her mind, betrayed their friendship.

He looked up at her and, reaching across the table, took her hand in his. "Let's walk for a while."

He pulled her up from the chair. The sun was just starting to sink below the hills, making the sky light up with some of her favorite colors. The hay in the fields had just been cut the week before and was being dried in large piles until they could be baled. The smell and sights were that of home, and she realized she didn't want to be anywhere else on Earth.

They started walking towards the creek, but instead of stopping by the water, he turned and started walking along the sandy shore.

"When you told me that you thought you were pregnant"—he paused and looked over at her— "I went through a slew of emotions before I settled on excitement." He stopped and turned towards her. "I wanted you to be pregnant. I wanted our child."

She heard herself gasp as she realized she'd never once considered that option. She'd always thought that he was scared, never that he would want her to be pregnant.

"We never talked about it," he continued. "Never talked about having kids." He shook his head. "We were too young to even give it a thought, other than protection against it. When I sat down and thought about it, after the night you'd told me, I realized I was more excited than scared. I could imagine our son or daughter." He smiled and brushed his finger down her chin. "They would have your green eyes." He ran his hand down her hair. "We would have a small house, some horses, and cattle." He laughed. "A tire swing on an old oak tree." He shook his head and his eyes turned dull. "Then you told me it was a false alarm and I was shattered." He brushed a tear from her cheek. She couldn't explain it, but she had been torn as well. He leaned closer to her until their breaths mixed. "I wanted it so bad, then it was gone, and I didn't know what to do. You looked so relieved when you told me; I thought you didn't want children. Didn't want them then and with me. The next morning, I saw things the way you had—clearly. We were so young." He shook his head. "I didn't have a job or a future. How was I going to support a family?" He closed his eyes for a second and sighed. "I thought I was doing the right thing by giving us a chance to grow up a little. Then I was called overseas and realized how big of a fool I'd been." He brushed his hand over her face again and she held her breath. "I never should have left you. There wasn't a day that went by that I didn't think about you, about us. I told myself that if I survived, I would do everything I could to get back to you. To win you back and show you how much you meant to me. How much you mean to me."

She shook her head. "I just . . . I didn't . . ." She swallowed. She couldn't think. Her mind was whirling with everything he'd just told her. She pulled back and took a step away. Without saying a word, she turned and started walking fast away from him.

"Haley?" He called out and rushed over to her, keeping pace next to her. "Are you okay?"

She nodded, not wanting him to see the tears falling down her face. He had wanted to start a family with her. He'd wanted the baby just as much as she had. She stopped and turned on him.

"I thought you didn't want to start a family with me. I thought you didn't want me anymore."

"I know. I'm sorry." He took her hand.

"You left me because you thought I didn't want a family with you?" She shook her head. "We used to be good at communicating. We grew up telling each other everything." She reached up and touched his face. "You hurt me." She dropped her hand to his chest and grabbed his shirtfront in her fists. "Don't do it again." Then she was up on her toes, her mouth fused to his. She felt the shock of the heat between them, the zip that traveled down to her toes. Then his hands were on her, roaming over her skin as she yanked his shirt open, sending his buttons flying in all different directions.

"Haley, my god," he gasped, trying to slow her down. But she needed speed. She needed him now.

Shaking her head, she pulled him back until they stood next to a tall pile of hay. With shaky fingers, she reached down and pulled her tank top up over her head. She saw his eyes heat when he saw her exposed skin. His lips curved into a smile slowly.

"Beautiful." He reached down and pulled off his ruined shirt. Then he was standing next to her, his hands on her hips, his eyes on her skin. "I've dreamed about this moment for years. Forgive me if I don't go slow."

She shook her head. "No, I need the speed. I need you." She reached down and took his belt buckle in her fingers as he reached down to help. They both laughed when he tried to remove his boots and almost landed on his butt. Finally, he stood before her in the dying light of the day, gloriously naked.

She noticed the nasty scar that ran down his left thigh. She ran her fingers over the raised skin. "Later"—she looked up into his eyes— "you'll have to tell me about it."

When he nodded, she wrapped her arms around his shoulders. He had several more muscles than he had before. She played her fingers over them, enjoying the feel of his tan skin.

He gathered her skirt up, bunching it in his hands. He moved them until they lay on the soft hay as his hands roamed over her sensitive skin, causing her to moan as he kissed her.

"Wes. I need you." She moved her hips until his hands pulled her cotton panties aside. When his fingers touched her heated skin, she cried out and dug her nails into his shoulders.

"My god," he gasped, "I've missed this."

Then she pulled at his boxers until her fingers wrapped around his length and she started to stroke him. His head fell back as he moaned.

He pulled her skirt up higher, trailing his mouth slowly down her skin, taking first one, then the other nipple into his mouth. He moved down her body until his shoulders rested on the insides of her thighs. He kissed her wet skin, using his tongue to send her to a place she'd forgotten. Her fingers went to his hair, holding onto his scalp as he pleasured her with his lips and fingers. He took his time, enjoying her, pleasing her, his fingers going deeper into her as his tongue played with the tight nub, rolling it between his lips and nibbling it gently with his teeth.

She closed her eyes and let the feeling of pleasure build inside her. It had been so long, too long since she'd felt anything like this. When she cried out his name, he hovered above her with a smile, knowing it was the first release of many to come.

"You taste just as I remembered." He leaned back and slid on the condom she hadn't known he'd opened. "My god, I've missed you, Haley Marie." He bent down and kissed her as he moved his hips slowly and slid into her heat.

He was bigger than she remembered, or maybe it was that her inner muscles hadn't been used in six years, but she gasped at the fullness of it all. When he moved slowly, the pleasure was undeniable. Her booted legs wrapped around his bare hips as she held on, thrust after thrust.

With one hand, he reached up and cupped her breast. Dipping his head, he tasted her skin and lapped at her nipple. When the cool evening air hit the wet skin, she moaned with pleasure as his hot mouth moved over her. His hips slowed a little until she grabbed them and dug her nails into his butt, causing him to move faster. He chuckled a little until she rotated her hips, moving him below her until she looked down at him.

Strands of hay floated down from her hair unnoticed as she straddled his hips. "Being overseas, you must have forgotten the speed us cowgirls like." She moved her hips as he smiled.

"Yes ma'am, why don't you show me." His smile was wicked. His fingers dug into her hips as she moved faster over him. She watched his eyes roam over her skin; his hands followed the path until she almost lost track of her pace. Her hips jolted when he thrust upward on his own, meeting and matching her movements.

When she heard him growl, she slid deeper and took her pleasure just as he took his own release.

❄

There was a thick strand of hay poking him in the butt, but he didn't care. Haley's naked body lay over his, her soft chest tight up against his own. Her legs were still wrapped around his hips, her core pressed to his. He was still buried deep inside her. He could feel her heartbeat and her breathing slow as he ran his hands up and down her back. Her long hair was getting in his face, but he didn't mind. Just the smell of her caused him to stir again.

She'd been so much more than he'd remembered. Her skin was softer than anything he'd ever felt. She smelled like heaven and tasted like spring. He doubted he could get enough of her in one lifetime.

Running his hands down to her hips, he held her still as he rotated up, pushing deeper into her. He felt her gasp against his chest and when he did it again, she moaned.

"Please," she whispered.

"Again?" he asked softly.

When she nodded, he rotated their positions until she lay underneath him, her dark hair fanned out on the soft hay.

"You are more beautiful than I remembered." He leaned down and placed a soft kiss on her lips. He wanted to go slow this time. He wanted a soft bed; he wanted to take his time with her, enjoying being inside her all night, until the sun came up.

"Here," he said, pulling back and wrapping his ruined shirt around her shoulders.

"What?" Her eyes flew open as he laughed.

"I want you in my bed. Tonight. All night." He shifted and picked her up. She was lighter than he remembered, and he easily carried her the few yards back to his small place.

By the time he pushed the door open, she had wrapped her arms around his shoulders and was raining kisses over his neck and face. He found it very hard to walk the few feet needed to his bed and ended up tripping a few times along the way.

When he laid her down on the bed, he noticed that they were both covered in hay and smiled. Kneeling beside her, he ran his fingers gently over her skin. Her eyes slid closed and her lips opened a little. Leaning down, he placed a kiss on her belly. He felt her breath hitch as he trailed his mouth along the line he'd traveled earlier.

"I can't seem to get enough of your taste." He trailed a finger around her belly button. "If I bottled it, I would easily become a millionaire." He smiled.

She giggled, then gasped when his lips touched her nether lips. Using his tongue, he parted her lips and niggled until he felt her hips jolt against his mouth. "More," he growled, pushing his fingers deep into her until he tasted her sweet nectar on his tongue.

Hovering over her, he waited until her breathing slowed a little until her eyes opened, and he saw the sea-green focus. Then he plunged into her in one swift motion, make her moan and gasp at the same time. Her nails dug into his shoulders, her legs wrapped tightly around his hips as he thrust harder and faster until they both lost the last of their control.

The dream came like it always did. Even with Haley's sweet body wrapped around his, the nightmare took hold and ripped at his mind.

Sights and sounds were blasting in his mind, causing his body to jerk and react. In his mind, he was trapped under the large metal beam, his friends, his team, all lying dead next to him from the initial blast. He was trying like mad to move the beam from his leg, but it wouldn't budge. Then he heard the men. He didn't know what they were saying, but he knew they were moving closer.

His weapon had been thrown a few feet away when the blast had ripped through the room. Sweat trickled down his back as he struggled to free himself.

They were coming to see if the homemade grenade had done its job. Looking around quickly, he realized everyone in his unit was dead. Everyone except him.

The men walked closer. He could hear them laughing as they discovered the first body. He heard them rummaging through his squad leader's belongings. The large beam blocked his view, but he could hear as the men moved closer, stopping at each of his team member's bodies, removing anything they found of value. When they stopped at Tracey's body, he watched through slits in his eyes as they ripped her clothing off. The four men looked at her naked body and made jokes, laughing and poking her bare breast with the end of their long rifles.

He felt his stomach revolt. Closing his eyes, he tried to block out everything in his mind. He was thankful she was gone. He was thankful she didn't have to suffer. None of them had suffered. It had happened too fast.

Then he heard one of the men stand above him. His body went limp as they pulled the watch his father had given him as a going-away present off his wrist. Someone kicked his ribs and spoke to the group. He forced himself not to breathe, not to make a sound as they rummaged through his bag, which was still attached to his chest. When the man couldn't open it, he called to the other men to help him pull it off his shoulders.

During the process, they had moved the beam enough that his leg was freed. Opening his eyes just a slit, he saw that the man who was trying to open his bag had set his weapon down right next to him. It took less than a second for him to react. First, he shot the one who was hovering above him in the eye, then the one who was standing behind his friend, taking the last two out as they ran to help their friends.

When it was all over, he sat with his back against the beam, blood running out of the large gash on his left leg. Five of his best friends lay lifeless on the dirt floor and the four men who had killed them were dead or bleeding to death.

He started to crawl over to the radio, so he could call for help. When he moved one of the attackers, he realized the man was no older than fifteen. When the kid's eyes flew open just as he leaned over him to grab the radio, he noticed how green they were.

Waking with a jolt, he realized it was Haley's green eyes staring down at him. The light on his nightstand was on and she'd pulled on one of his old shirts and sweat shorts. She sat cross-legged next to him, her hands resting on his shoulders like she'd been shaking him.

He ran his hands over his face and sat up. "Sorry, did I wake you?"

She nodded. "It was a bad one." The worried look in her eyes said it all.

Usually, his dreams didn't lock him in that long. The

nightmares almost always ended before the men had searched him.

"Are you okay?" she asked, scooting closer to him on the bed.

He nodded and glanced over at the alarm clock. Why was it always the same time? He sighed and leaned his head back against the headboard. Keeping his eyes closed, he reached for her and pulled her down next to him.

"Just let me hold you for a while. It's too late to explain and I don't want to keep you up for the rest of the night."

She snuggled next to him and ran her hands over his chest slowly. "I don't mind. If you want to talk about it."

He looked down at her and smiled slightly. "I know you won't rest until you hear it." He chuckled when she nodded and rested her head against his chest.

By the time he was done telling his story, she was sitting up, looking deep into his eyes, concern written all over her face.

"What happened next?"

He shook his head. "I don't remember much. I blacked out when the kid pushed me off him. When I woke, the radio was lying next to me and the kid was gone. I was airlifted to the hospital, then to the VA in Germany where I spent the next month learning how to walk again."

"I'm sorry you went through all that." She leaned back against him again. Then reached up and kissed him. "I'm thankful you survived."

He nodded. "I dream every night. Nothing I do seems to stop it from coming." He closed his eyes, afraid to tell her that he'd hoped the dreams would stop when he was with her.

"It may just take time." She ran her hands over his chest. His hand rested over hers.

"I suppose." He scooted them down further until they were lying side by side. His ran his hands underneath her T-shirt until she moaned and started moving under his hands.

CHAPTER 7

When Haley walked back to the house the next morning, she couldn't keep her mind off the differences she'd seen and felt in Wes. He wasn't the same boy he was when he left almost six years ago, and she wasn't just talking physically.

Hearing his experiences had opened her eyes to the fact that he'd been through so much more than she had over the course of their being apart. She couldn't explain what it did to her, hearing what he'd endured. She'd seen the limp. The whole town had. Since his folks weren't big on gossip, everyone speculated about what had happened. Nothing had come close to the story he'd told her last night.

She'd missed having him around, being with him. He used to be the only person she could talk to for hours and hours without feeling strange about it. They would talk about their hopes and dreams, about the places they would travel to, about anything and everything.

Could they be that again? He'd been through so many

things and had grown so much that she was starting to feel like she hadn't moved an inch since he'd left Fairplay.

Did they even really have anything in common anymore other than physical attraction? Her mind flashed to what he'd done to her after he'd told her that story. Of what they'd done before. Her cheeks heated, and her body responded to just the thought of him. She was so embarrassed, thinking that one of her sisters would see it, that she slipped into the barn and up to her thinking spot, only to find Lauren and Chase up there, looking guilty. Chase was tucking his shirt in and Lauren had straw in her hair.

"Well, well, well." Haley leaned against the post and crossed her arms over her chest. "Having a little fun in the hay are we?"

Chase laughed as Lauren looked embarrassed and started making excuses.

"There was a . . ." She looked at her husband.

"Mouse," he suggested

"Yes, a mouse. I saw it and fell back and Chase—"

"Caught it with my shirt and tossed it outside." Chase smiled, going along with his wife's game.

"Yes," Lauren glared at Chase. "Anyway, I better get back to—"

"Work?" Haley suggested for her.

"Yes." Lauren quickly walked out as Chase and Haley laughed.

"She's no good at that," Haley said, walking over to her thinking spot and sitting down.

Chase just laughed. "I know, but it's one of the reasons I love her so much." He walked over and sat across from her. "I guess since I know her so well, I can tell when one of her sisters has something on her mind. And don't think I don't see that hay in your hair too." She reached up to her hair before remembering that she'd showered at Wes's place. Chase laughed and pointed at her. "Caught you. So, how as your dinner with Wes anyway?"

She laughed and leaned back. "Fine." Then she shrugged her shoulders. "I don't know. I thought it was fine. I mean, he told me why he left."

Chase's eyebrows shot up in question.

"I mean . . ." She blushed, remembering no one had known of their scare before graduation.

Chase shook his head. "Oh, no. You can't hide that one from me." He smiled. "Remember, I can read you now, too."

She sighed. "Fine, but you have to promise not to tell anyone else."

He laughed. "I promise." When she just looked at him, he continued, "Remember, I did keep Lauren's and my marriage a secret for seven years."

She smiled. "Yes, and we are all still upset at you for it."

"It all worked out fine and I'm where I'm supposed to be now." He leaned back and rested his shoulders on a bale of hay. "So, spill."

She took a deep breath and blurted it out. "Six years ago, before Wes signed up for the army, I thought I was pregnant. But when it turned out to be a false alarm, he joined the military and left. I thought it was because he didn't want a family, didn't want me, but it turns out he was heartbroken because he thought I didn't want a family with him." She grabbed her head. "Wow, it sounded a lot better in my head."

Chase just looked at her.

"Okay, I know it was stupid. We were young and well . . . stupid, but we used to tell each other everything. Then," she shrugged her shoulders again, "something that big got between us and we stopped."

"Do you think you can pick up where you left off?" he asked.

She shook her head.

"Good," he stood and dusted off his jeans.

"Good?" She stood and looked at him. "What does that mean?"

"Don't think that you can start where you left off, because you can't. You can never go back to the way it was when you were kids. Trust me. You're two different people now." He walked over to her and took her shoulders in his hands. "But you can start new. Take it from me." He smiled. "If you don't, you'll be missing out on all the fun." He gave her a brotherly hug and then smiled. "Now, I guess I'd better get back to . . ." He smiled.

"Work." She laughed.

About an hour before nightfall, she'd convinced herself that she was over-thinking everything. She sat out on the back deck and ate barbeque ribs with Lauren, Chase, Grant, and Alex and felt a little better. She was cutting the watermelon that had come from Alex's new garden when Wes walked up on the back deck.

"Something smells wonderful." He smiled and walked over to shake Grant's and Chase's hands.

When she looked up at him, she was so focused on watching the way he moved, that she didn't realize that she'd cut her finger until Alex gasped.

"Haley!" Alex rushed over. "You're bleeding all over

my watermelon." Alex grabbed a white towel and wrapped it around her finger.

"Oh!" Then she felt the sting and sucked in her breath with the pain.

Looking down, she saw the blood on her tan shirt and groaned. "Great, another shirt ruined."

Wes was beside her. "Are you hurt?" He took her hand from Alex and examined it. Chase, being the only person with actual medical knowledge, walked over and glanced at the cut.

"She'll live." He nodded to Wes. "My medical bag is on top of the fridge. There's some antiseptic and clean gauze in it."

Wes nodded and pulled Haley through the back door.

"I can take care of a little cut myself," she started to say but was hushed by Wes as he reached up with one hand to grab Chase's bag. His other hand was still holding her cut closed with the towel. "Come over here." He pulled her towards the table. He pushed lightly on her shoulder with the bag until she sat down on the edge of the table.

Pulling out a small bottle, he doused her cut with the stinky brown liquid quickly, causing her to hiss with pain. When she tried to jerk her hand away, Wes held it still until he was satisfied that the cut was clean. Then he used another clean towel to dry her hand before wrapping her finger tightly.

"There." He looked up at her and smiled, the concern leaving his face. "All patched up."

She frowned at him. "Your bedside manner could use some work."

He smiled and spoke softly. "I'm sorry." He stepped between her knees as she sat on the table. "They didn't teach us how to kiss a boo-boo in the army." He laughed when she made a face. "But for you . . ." He dropped off as their lips met. "I can learn."

"Is everything okay in here?" Lauren asked, walking in with little Ricky on her hip. The boy was cute as a button in his little shorts and button-up shirt. He'd kicked one of his boots off earlier and now was trying to get the other one off by banging his foot against his mother's hip. His chubby fingers reached out towards Haley as Lauren walked into the room.

Haley had been playing with Ricky ever since they'd gone out in the backyard, but the kid couldn't get enough of his aunt.

Pushing on Wes's shoulder until he moved aside, she jumped off the table and reached for her nephew. "There's my favorite boy. Come give your favorite auntie a kiss." She kissed his cheeks until the boy squealed with laughter.

Wes and Lauren followed them outside. "You'll stay for dinner; Chase has made enough ribs to feed an army," Lauren said as they walked outside.

"Well," Wes smiled, "it smells and sounds so good. Just don't let Haley anywhere near the watermelon again."

It was nice sitting on the back deck talking to her family. They tried to get together at least once a week. They would have liked to do it more, but Alex and Lauren still worked at Mama's diner, occasionally.

When she looked across the table at Wes, she couldn't help but seeing how well he fit in with her family. The guys joked back and forth with each other while the women talked about the progress Ricky was making in life.

The little boy was going on two years old and was

smarter than most kids twice his age. At least according to his mother and aunts. Ricky had been blessed with the West green eyes and his father's jet-black hair. The mix was something to see in a chubby toddler.

After dinner, Ricky walked around the table and ended up sitting in Wes's lap. His face and fingers had been wiped clean by his father, but he still managed to spill some sauce on Wes's shirt. Wes didn't seem to mind or notice it. He just played peek-a-boo with the little boy and melted Haley's heart a little bit more.

After the sun went down, they sat on the swing on the back deck and talked some more. She still felt like she was holding herself back from him, but she couldn't explain why. After all, he'd gone through so much and had even taken the time to explain his past actions.

But, to date, he hadn't once talked about the future. She didn't know if he was ready to talk to her or not, but she did know that she wasn't going to completely trust him until he told her his plans.

It wasn't as if she was asking for much. After all, she didn't think she could explain her future plans to anyone if they asked. She'd been born and raised on Saddleback ranch. The longest she'd been away from it had been the one summer her father had gotten it in his mind to send her to riding camp. It was the most grueling week she'd ever spent. She couldn't remember ever being so homesick in her life.

It was getting a little difficult living with Lauren and Chase. They had started their own family and planned on expanding it even further. Alex had married Grant and moved out over a year ago, so that helped. It was a big house, but Haley was starting to realize just how small it felt when you were constantly walking in on a couple who wanted privacy. She tried to joke with them about it and always tried really hard to avoid areas she knew they were in. But bumping into them like today was inevitable.

More and more over the last year, she had wondered what she was going to do about it. She knew she wasn't ready to marry. Up until Wes had returned, she'd only found one other man in town worthy of dating.

Finally, Wes stood up and explained that he had to be in Tyler first thing in the morning. She didn't pry, and he didn't explain why, which only made it harder to trust him again.

When he kissed her goodnight, she felt that he was holding something back. As she watched him walk away, she felt like crying.

Why had she let herself walk into this again? She was so torn; she didn't know what to do. Maybe some time away would help? She had some cousins she could go spend some time with. They lived about an hour away and she always had a fun time on their ranch. They ran a horse ranch, something she'd always dreamed of doing but had never had the time or money to.

Leaning her head back against the swing, she closed her eyes and imagined her future. She dreamed of what she would want to do if time and money weren't a problem.

She'd name the ranch Haley's Sanctuary. She wouldn't just stop at horses. Her sanctuary would be open to all different kinds of animals: horses, cows, goats, dogs, even llamas. She stopped swinging and smiling. The Becker's down the road had a few llamas. She always loved working with them. They were mischievous, but very smart creatures.

She wondered where in Fairplay she could open such a ranch. There weren't too many places in town, but she knew of a few older ranches on the outskirts that could be fixed up to house such a large endeavor.

By the time she walked upstairs to head to bed, she had it all planned out in her mind. All she needed now was money and time.

The next few days she had little of either. What she had plenty of was sweat and blood. She had ripped open the cut on her finger several times while cleaning out stalls or helping with the cattle. Even though she wore gloves, every evening she would walk in, her hand covered in blood.

"Damn." She was standing in the kitchen covered in hay and dirt, looking down at her bloody hand.

"Damn, damn, damn," Ricky's sweet voice came from behind her.

She turned and winced at Lauren. "Sorry, I didn't know you were behind me."

Lauren shook her head and frowned at Haley's hand. "Is that thing still bothering you?"

"Yeah, it just won't close up. I've cleaned it and bandaged it up. But you know how it is when you use your hands the way we do."

Lauren nodded. She sat Ricky in his high chair, making sure to lock him in. He was a master of escape and everyone joked that they should have called him Houdini instead. "Here, try this." Lauren walked to the kitchen cabinet and pulled out a small bottle just as Alex walked in the back door.

"Super glue?" she asked Lauren.

Her sister nodded. "Trust me." Then she turned to

Alex, who was still dressed in her uniform from Mama's. "Busy day?"

"You've no idea," Alex said, sitting down next to Ricky.

"Damn, damn, damn," Ricky said, smiling as he banged his hands on his high chair.

Alex laughed as Haley cringed. "I win the bet." Alex looked over at Lauren and held out her hand to Haley.

"Bet? What bet?" Lauren asked.

"Nothing," Haley said quickly. She reached into her purse and handed her sister a twenty.

"Haley Marie. What the . . ."—Lauren looked towards her son— ". . . moon, are you talking about?"

"We bet on who would be the first to teach your son curse words," Alex said, holding up the twenty. "And you can see by the dollar signs in my eyes and the crisp bill in my hands that I won. I won. I won." Alex got up off the chair and did a little dance, much to Ricky's delight. He started clapping his hands and singing, "I won," too.

Lauren laughed. "At least he's not saying . . . the other word anymore."

Haley spent the next few minutes cleaning up her hand and trying to super-glue her finger back together. By the time she tossed the small bottle on the table, several of her fingers were glued together.

Alex sat back and watched her, laughing at first, then reached over and started to help. Seeing her sister's blonde head bent over her hand, a flash of memory played in Haley's head.

Haley didn't really remember their mother well; she was only four when the tornado took her away. But seeing

Alex's head bent over her hand, she was sure that her mother had done something similar.

"Haley?" Lauren asked from across the room. "What is it?" Her sister rushed to her side.

"Hale?" Alex looked up at her. Her dark chocolate eyes turned a deeper shade, widened a little, and her face softened. For a split second, she could see her mother's face instead of Alex's.

"Mom," she croaked out, her voice going hoarse with the emotions. "I remember mom doing this."

"What?" Alex had a frown on her face. "Hal, you're white as a sheet. Lauren, call that husband of yours inside."

Lauren rushed to the back door, only to be stopped by Haley. "No, wait. I'm okay, really. I just—it's just that I remembered Mom." She smiled a little. "For the first time in my life, I remembered Mom."

"Oh, sweetie." Lauren rushed to her sister's side, bent down, and hugged her.

Tears were streaming down Haley's face. She could feel her sisters hugging her and even felt Ricky's little hand reach out and tug her hair. Closing her eyes, she played the scene in her memory over again, wanting to hold onto it.

"I had a boo-boo." She pulled back and smiled at her sister's face. "Here." She held up her thumb. "Mom was putting an Elmo Band-Aid on it. I wanted a rainbow one, but Alex had used them all on her dolly earlier." She frowned at Alex, who only smiled and shrugged her shoulders.

"Dolly had a lot of boo-boos that summer."

"Mom's head was bent down, looking at my boo-boo. She was singing to me. The 'All Better' song."

Alex looked off towards the window and started singing, her rich voice laced with country as she sang her mother's original song.

"I know you're scared
But I will always be there
I know there's pain
But I'll hold you til it goes away
I'll kiss it all better, (ooo)
I'll kiss it all better (ooo)
I will always be there for you
Cause that's just what mammas do
There's no need for you to cry
Cause you're the apple of your mamma's eye
I'll kiss it all better (ooo)
Kiss it all better
Just for you, I'll kiss it all better"

When Alex was done singing, there were even more tears in the kitchen as the sisters hugged one another.

"You sound so much like her," Lauren said. "It's not fair." Her sister smiled and held Alexis's face. "You get her looks, her voice, and from what dad always said her temperament."

They all laughed just as Chase walked in the back door.

"What going on?" When he saw the tears, he had the face all men get when they walk into a room full of weeping women. His eyes darted around the room and found a dozen escape routes. The sisters laughed as they hugged and cried.

Wes threw the cane against the door. He hadn't wanted the damn surgery. There was no way he was going to go back to walking with a damn stick. When the pretty nurse walked back in, she looked down at the cane and frowned.

"Now, Mr. Tanner, this isn't going to do you any good clear over here." Not even her southern drawl and pretty smile could lift his spirits.

"I don't want the damn thing." He started to stand up and almost toppled over. The nurse raced across the small space and wrapped her arms around his hips. If he hadn't been so focused on his pain, he would have appreciated the nice pair of breasts pushed tightly against his chest.

Hell, he had to be honest with himself. Ever since he'd come home, there was only one pair of breasts his mind had been on—Haley's.

Now he'd gone and ruined his chances with her. What was she going to think of him when he hobbled back into town tomorrow? What could he say? Oh, hey, by the way, I just had major surgery without telling you, and I'll need at least two more in the next year.

Great, just great. He closed his eyes as the nurse forced him to sit back on the table. "Mr. Tanner, if you continue to do reckless things, you're going to end up on the floor, and I'll have to call an orderly." She leaned forward and whispered to him. "And they aren't near as nice as I am." She winked and handed him his cane. "Now, shall we try this again?"

The next day, he sat in his father's truck and leaned his head back. There were a million excuses running through his head. None of them explained why he'd kept this secret from the town. Why he didn't want the support of the people he loved. Maybe it was his parents' fault? He looked over at his dad. He was the spitting image of his old man, except that his dad had silver hair and a little beer gut.

His parents kept to themselves as much as they could, which was hard in such a small town. But they kept to themselves and liked it that way. Maybe that's why he hadn't told anyone what he was going through.

Closing his eyes, he knew excuses wouldn't cut it with Haley. He should have told her.

When his father drove up to the small house, he cringed when he saw her sitting out on his front porch.

"I'm sorry. I know you didn't want anyone to know what was going on." His father looked over at him as he cut the engine. "But your mother thought it was best that someone knows you would be needing some help. Since you're living here," he nodded, "we thought it best that someone close check up on you for a few days."

He nodded. "Thanks, Dad."

His father opened his door and rushed around to open it for him. Haley was there, holding her hands in front of her. He could tell by the look in her eyes that she was worried but couldn't read anything more. She stood there as his father helped him into his house.

He sat on the couch, his cane propped up next to him, feeling a little light headed. He hated the medication he'd been given and had even protested against taking it. But in the end, his doctor and the pain had won out.

"Well, I'll leave you in her capable hands." His father handed Haley the small white bag of his medications, which Wes had no intention of taking for very long.

"Thanks for the lift, Dad." He rested his head back when his father walked out.

"How are you feeling?" Haley asked, sitting down in the chair opposite him.

"Fine, really. It's no big deal. I don't know why they called you. I hope you didn't worry."

"Worry?" Her eyebrows shot up. "You didn't give me a chance to worry. By the time I found out about all this, you were already on your way here." Her voice was laced with pain. "Your mother said your surgery was three days ago. Is that correct?" She crossed her hands on her lap. When he nodded, she closed her eyes and sighed. When her eyes opened back up, he saw the pain.

"Haley, I'm sorry I didn't—"

"Don't." She stood up. "No more apologies." She picked up the bag of medicine again. "I won't listen to them anymore." She turned and walked into the kitchen. He could hear her getting him a glass of water, then she was walking back in, the pills and water in her hands.

"It says you have to take this when you get home." She held them out. "Then every four hours until the pain is bearable."

"It's bearable now." He pushed the pills away, but took the water and gulped it down, hoping the pain was masked enough.

"Don't lie to me." She stood over him. "Don't be dumber than you've already been. Take the damn pills so I can make you some dinner without worrying."

"You don't have to stick around." He took the pills, knowing that she would force it down his throat if he didn't take them. He hated that the pills made him loopy. The first hour of the drive home, he'd been talking about how cool butterflies were. To his father! He certainly didn't want Haley to witness him like that.

"What did they do?"

"Hmm?" he asked, wishing she would sit down next to him so he could see her green eyes. He'd dreamed about them last night in his hospital bed as the medicine ran through his veins.

She sat next to him, putting her hand on his. "Why did you need surgery?"

Maybe the pills were already kicking in, but she looked softer, sexier.

"There was a blood vessel that was blocked. They had to replace it. Sorta."

"What?" She looked shocked. "Replace it?"

"Yeah," he laughed. "They took some from my good leg"—he motioned to his upper thigh— "then stitched it to here." He pointed to his injured leg. "Bam." He slapped his hands together, almost missing. "I'll be as good as new, or so they say." His words started to slur, and his head fell back again. "Damn, I hate being loopy." He rolled his head towards her and looked at her and smiled. He tried to reach up towards her, but she was too far away. "You are so beautiful. I can't believe how much I love you."

CHAPTER 8

es's eyes closed, and he began to snore lightly.

"You are so beautiful. I can't believe how much I love you."

His words played over and over in her mind as she watched him sleep. If he really loved her, why did she have to find out about his surgery from his parents? Three days later!

She'd been hurt when he'd left without telling her why he was going out of town. Not that she was one of those girlfriends who needed to know where her man was at all times.

She didn't even really think of them as dating again. After all, they had just gotten together once. It wasn't as if he'd made any commitments to her, yet.

She stood up and walked into his kitchen to make him some soup. The hospital instructions stated that he should eat light tonight. Banging around his kitchen, she found the makings for some homemade chicken soup, something she was a pro at making. She enjoyed cooking. It was one of the first things Haley and her sisters learned to do to help out after their mom died. Their father was a wonderful father, rancher, and even seamstress, but he couldn't cook to save his life.

By the time the place smelled of warm chicken soup and French bread, she could hear Wes in the next room. She walked in with a tray full of food for him and almost spilled it all when she saw him trying to stand without his cane.

"What are you doing?" She gasped and set the tray down quickly. Racing over, she wrapped her arms around him quickly, just before he started to fall backward.

"Damn," he said into her hair as he used all his weight to hold himself up. "Stupid leg." She helped him walk towards the table and sit down.

"Don't do that again," she scolded. "You could have eaten on the couch."

He shook his head. "I'm tired of eating in bed or on a couch. I wanted to have dinner with you." He reached over and took her hand. "With candles." He nodded towards the candles he'd used last week. "Will you light them again?"

"Why?" she asked, looking down at his face. She could see that his brown eyes were still clouded, and he was a little paler than normal.

"Because you look so beautiful in candlelight." He reached up and brushed her hair with the back of his hand. "Please."

She sighed and proceeded to light the dozen candles. Then she walked over and flipped off the dining room light. Taking her tray, she set the two bowls of soup down in front of them, then set the bread down.

"It smells like heaven." He leaned down and stuck his nose right in front of the soup, almost dipping the tip in it. She leaned over and pushed him back up.

"You're still loopy, aren't you?"

He nodded and tried to pick up his spoon. On the second try, he got it. "I hate those drugs. I told the doctor they did funny things to me." It took him a few tries to finally get a spoonful of liquid.

She took his hand before he spilled the entire spoonful all over himself. "Here, let me help you."

He looked up and smiled at her. "You are so beautiful. You taste so wonderful, too."

She chuckled at that. "Thanks, I think." She scooped a spoonful into his mouth and watched his eyes close.

"Mmmm, I can't believe how good this is. Almost as good as licking you from head to toe." He smiled.

She laughed. "You are incorrigible."

"As long as I'm around you, I am." He took another bite she offered.

"Here, have some bread."

He took the bread from her and nibbled on it.

"I don't want you to leave me." He frowned. "Please say you'll stay."

She thought about it, and after seeing what the pills were doing to him, doubted he could be left alone anytime soon. It didn't mean that she was going to sleep in his bed, but she wasn't going to leave him alone.

"Yes, I'll stay tonight."

She shook his head. "Stay." He reached across the table and took her hand. "Please. Don't leave."

She nodded. "Yes."

He smiled. "Good, I have big plans you know."

Her eyebrows shot up. "Oh?"

"Yes, but I can't tell you yet. Soon." He took another bite of his bread. "Soon."

After she'd fed him half a bowl of soup and a full roll of bread, she helped him walk back to his bed, where he fell back and dropped quickly asleep.

She had to push his legs up on the bed, carefully. He was wearing shorts, something he never really wore. His left leg had a white bandage wrapped around his thigh. She itched to see what was going on underneath it but knew that it needed to heal first.

There was a smaller bandage on his right upper thigh. Pulling it back gently, she saw the small incision where they had, most likely, removed a small section of his vein to fix his other leg. She didn't know much about the procedure and decided to step outside and call Chase to see if he knew anything more about it.

Chase informed her that it was a pretty standard surgery. Depending on the extent of the damage, he would most likely be off his feet for a few weeks. But after recovering, he would notice an increase in color and strength in that leg. There were high chances of it healing quickly and minimal risks now that the surgery was over.

He told her that if she had any problems, to let him know and he could be there quickly.

After assuring him that she'd keep Wes off his feet for the next few days, she hung up, wondering what she was going to do now.

She ended up snuggling down on his couch and watching an old movie. She even made popcorn and drank some of the wine that was left over from their dinner last week.

She must have fallen asleep, but she jolted awake when she heard Wes screaming. Rushing to his room, she saw him sitting straight up in bed, his eyes wide. His hands were flailing about, and when she flipped on the lights, she could see that he was still trapped in the nightmare.

"Wes!" she called out over and over as she tried to calm him down, holding him still so he wouldn't hurt himself or her.

He kept screaming until she softly touched his face. "Wes." Tears were streaming down her face. "Please wake up."

She pulled him close as he went still.

"Haley?" She felt his arms wrap around her. "I'm sorry, baby. I'm so sorry. I love you so much. I can't believe I ever walked away from you. Please be real." He said it over and over again until she leaned up and kissed him on the lips.

"I'm real. I am real. I'm right here."

"Don't go away. Please don't ever leave me." He pulled her closer as they fell back onto the bed. She lay next to him, outside the covers, until she felt his breathing slow.

She knew he was asleep again and wished that she could go with him. But her mind was whirling as he held her tight. Even in sleep, he refused to let her go. His arms were wrapped around her, keeping her warm in the cool night air.

She thought of all the times they had been together physically and when she finally fell asleep, she dreamed of the first time they had made love.

When she woke, he wasn't in the bed. She was wrapped in the blanket. She'd removed her shoes in the living room, so her socked feet were starting to get hot as the sun streamed into the window and landed on the end of the bed.

Kicking off the blankets, she sat up and looked around. Seeing that his cane was no longer leaning against the wall by his bed, she smiled. At least he'd used it.

Walking towards the bathroom, she heard him splashing around in the sink.

"I hope you aren't drowning in there," she called out.

"Nope, but you can come in and watch, just in case," he called out.

She laughed. "How about I start some breakfast. When you're washed up, call me and I'll help you walk in."

"Okay, I'll be just a few more minutes."

She walked into the kitchen, stretching her arms over her head as she went. She felt like making blueberry pancakes but doubted he had any fresh fruit around. Opening the freezer, she smiled when she saw the large bag of frozen blueberries.

By the time he walked in, minus the cane, she had a batch of blueberry pancakes, scrambled eggs, and turkey sausage cooked up.

She had made a pitcher of orange juice and was sipping some coffee as she set the table.

"Mmm smells great." She could see that his eyes were clearer and even though she saw the pain in his face, she decided to let him judge if he needed more pills today.

"How are you feeling?"

"Great, and before you ask, no, I don't want any more pills." He smiled as he sat down. She saw him cringe a little, but he recovered quickly. When he looked up at her again, he smiled like nothing had happened.

"I'll trust you, so long as you let Chase swing by today."

"Chase?" He laughed. "Now I'm seeing a vet, too."

She chuckled. "I trust him completely with all my animals." She set a full plate in front of him. "Now eat up."

"Yes, ma'am." He smiled as he scooped up a spoonful of eggs.

Five days later, Wes stood next to a horse that was all saddled up as Lauren, Alex, and Haley glared down at him.

"No," all three of them said at the same time.

"But—" he started, only to be interrupted by the word again. "Chase said—" he started, but they repeated their refusal. "Really?" He tossed down the reins, almost feeling like a child.

The horse, for his part, started walking towards the barn again. Wes stopped the old guy several times, but each time he was confronted by the wall that was the West sisters.

He was so tired of being cooped up in the house; he just wanted to go for a ride. Chase had told him he could go if he rode Dash, didn't go faster than a slow walk and stayed in the front field.

But so far, the sisters refused to listen to their vet. He bet that even if he had a signed note from his human doctor, they wouldn't let him on a horse for another week.

He crossed his arms over his chest. "When?"

Haley hopped down from the black horse she was on

and walked over to him. Taking him by the shoulders, she started walking towards the back deck. She smiled and said softly, "Next week you have a doctor's appointment on Monday. If he clears you, then we can go for a long, slow ride."

Images flooded his mind: Haley wrapping her long legs around his hips, her hat and boots still on, with nothing else.

"Earth to Wes?" Haley said, laughing. "Where did you go just then?"

He smiled. "Where do you think?" he said, pulling her into the shade of a large oak. Here the shade was thick, and the breeze was cool. He pulled her up against the large tree trunk and kissed her slowly.

"I see you're feeling better." She smiled as she rubbed her hip against the bulge in his jeans.

"Never better. Stop by tonight and—"

"Haley! Help!" Alex screamed from across the yard.

Haley looked over just in time to see Lauren start to slide off her horse, just a few feet away. Wes rushed as fast as he could, but he was too late to catch her sister before she hit the ground. Haley had made it in time to be knocked down by her bigger sister.

"What the—?" He rushed over just as Chase came riding up. Chase's feet hit the ground before his horse stopped.

"Damn it! I told her not to get on a horse today." He rushed over and took his wife into his arms. Looking up at Alex, he said, "Water. Now!"

By the time Alex came back with a large glass of water, Lauren was already sitting up, apologizing.

"What the hell is wrong?" Alex blurted out. "She can't be pregnant. She barfs, not faints."

Chase laughed. "Well, this time she faints."

"What?" Haley and Alex said at the same time. "Wait. What!"

Chase smiled up at his two sisters-in-law and nodded. "Looks like the cat's out of the bag now. I told her not to ride today. Him on the other hand, I told could ride." He nodded towards Wes.

Wes smiled and nodded, crossing his arms over his chest. Then worry filled his mind. "Is she okay?"

Lauren nodded. "Just bruised my pride. I haven't fallen off a horse since I was ten."

"It could be twins," Haley put in with a smile. Lauren glared at her from her spot in the dirt. It was a running joke with her and her sisters. Twins ran in the family, and she knew it was just a matter of hitting the winning ticket. Maybe that's why Lauren was fainting now instead?

"That's it for today," Chase said, picking Lauren up before she could stand. "You are on bed rest until these spells stop." He started walking towards the house as Lauren wrapped her arms around his neck. He looked over his shoulder. "Since we're short two people, hop on Dash and take it easy," he told Wes.

By the end of the workday, Wes was wondering why he'd wanted to get on a horse so soon after surgery in the first place.

His thighs hurt at his incision points. Hell, even his groin was pounding like a mother. He knew he was going to be covered in bruises by tomorrow morning. When he hobbled back into his place, he threw a large bag of frozen peas on his crotch and watched the news from the couch.

He wished for a beer, but he'd forgotten to grab one on his way to the couch. When he felt himself nodding off, he walked into the kitchen, grabbed a fresh bag of peas, and fell into bed.

That night he dreamed of dark-haired babies with green eyes and his chin. He dreamed of a large spread filled with animals and children. The next morning, he was half showered before he realized the nightmare hadn't come last night.

For the first time in a year, he'd slept the whole night through without remembering, and it was all because of what he wanted for his future. Now he just needed to secure that future and persuade Haley to go along for the ride.

He spent the morning on the phone, trying to move his loan process ahead. The VA had approved the place he'd picked, but it seemed he needed more paperwork for the bank to guarantee the loan.

It was around noon when he drove away from his folks' place, a folder of needed paperwork next to him on the seat. He decided to swing by Mama's for some lunch and smiled when he saw Haley's car parked out front.

When he walked in, he saw her sitting in a back booth, a book pulled up close to her face. Waving at Alex as he walked by, he sat across from Haley and smiled when she looked up at him.

"How's it going?" He tilted his head and looked at the title of the book and the half-naked couple embracing on the cover. "Since when did you start reading these?" He plucked the book from her hands and glanced at the text. His eyebrows shot up and a smile crossed his face. When he looked back at Haley, he could see that her cheeks had turned a little pink.

She shrugged her shoulders and smiled a little. "Since you left."

"Hmmm, I wish they had these overseas." He laughed and set the book down just as Haley's food was delivered.

"What can I get you?" Alex asked.

He looked at what Haley had. The large turkey sandwich, complete with home fries and white gravy made his stomach growl loudly. "That looks great. I'll have the same."

"How are you feeling today?" Haley asked once her sister was gone.

"A little sore, but I'll survive." He handed the book back to her and leaned forward. "How about you swing by later tonight and we'll try . . . ." He tapped the book and winked. He was pleased to see her face flush even more.

"I can't tonight." She looked down at their joined hands. "I'm babysitting Ricky. Lauren and Chase are having a date night."

He smiled. "Well, how about I come over and keep you company?"

She looked at him. "There will be a two-year-old in the house."

He chuckled. "I can control my urges around the kid. It'll be fun."

She shook her head and smiled, "If you want to hang out with a two-year-old. I warn you, there will be Scooby Doo playing on the TV, toys all over the floor, and . . . ." She smiled. "Peanut butter and jelly for dinner."

"Sounds wonderful." He squeezed her hand, meaning it.

After lunch, he excused himself and left Haley in the diner. He walked across the street to the bank so he could hand deliver the paperwork they needed for his loan. When he walked through the glass doors, he inwardly groaned when he spotted Savannah standing in the short line.

When she saw him, her eyes lit up and she straightened her back so her breasts stuck out even more. She was wearing a red and white sundress that showcased what most men thought of as her best assets. Her red heels made them stand almost eye-to-eye. When he stepped closer to her, her rich perfume hit him full force. If he hadn't prepared for it, he would have coughed. He nodded as he walked up next to her to wait his turn to be helped.

"Well, what brings you into the bank today?" She grabbed his arm and ran her hand up and down his bicep.

"Paperwork." He held up the folder.

Her eyebrows shot up. "Oh, let me guess. For a loan"—her eyes got narrow— "for a new truck?"

He looked out the glass doors at his old truck and thought about getting a new one, but that would have to wait for a while. He shook his head.

He hated telling her, knowing that if he did, it would be all over town before nightfall that he was buying a house. So, he remained silent.

"Aren't you the secretive one?" She turned and frowned when she realized she was next in line. She let go of his arm when she was called up to the cashier. He thought he heard her sigh, but he tried to ignore the sound.

He waited for her to finish making a deposit, then groaned again when he realized she wasn't going to leave the small bank until he was done with his transaction. He walked up to Steven, the clerk, and nodded.

"Hey, Steve. Betty needed this paperwork from me."

"Hi, Wes. Betty stepped out for lunch. Would you like to wait for her?"

He shook his head, imagining sitting in the bank with Savannah to keep him company. "No, that's okay. If you can just give her this folder, I'll come back tomorrow and pick them back up."

"Okay." Steve took the folder. "I hear you're close to getting the old place on Bond Drive." Steve shook his head. "That old place still standing?"

Wes laughed. "Barely. I plan on tearing it down. Got a new double wide from the VA that's going to take its place, at least until I can build something of my own."

Steve whistled. "Joan and I finished our place last year." He shook his head. "Lot of work and money."

Wes laughed. "I bet. I drove by your place the other day. You'll have to give me the guy's name who did all the stonework for you."

Steve smiled. "My brother-in-law, Gary. Hang on, I'll write down his number for you."

Wes stood there, leaning against the counter, while Steve rushed to the back. He could feel Savannah's eyes on his back but jolted when her hand came to rest on his arm again.

"Why, shame on you, Wes." She rubbed her breast up against his arm. "Keeping a secret like that from me. You should take me up to the place sometime, show me around," she purred.

He was thankful when Steve came back, a card in his hand, and he didn't have to reply.

"Here. Bobby works for a company in Tyler, but if you mention my name, he'll do the work under the table."

"Thanks." Wes nodded and took the card.

"I'll make sure Betty gets this paperwork." Steve took up the folder. "Take care."

Wes stepped aside and tried to get past Savannah, but she just wrapped her arm in his and walked with him out of the bank, chatting about wanting to see the place on Bond Drive.

$\mathcal{H}$aley glanced up from her book and was shocked to see Wes walking out of the bank with Savannah on his arm. She laughed when she saw the uncomfortable look on his face.

"What's so funny?" Alex walked up and looked out the window. "Well, I never." Her sister sat across from her.

"Look at his face," Haley said, between laughs.

Alex started laughing. "He looks like he'd rather have his toenails pulled out slowly than be standing next to her."

They both watched as Savannah rubbed her large breast against his arm. No doubt she was purring and enjoying it all.

"You better go save him before he has a stroke right there on Main Street," Alex said, giggling.

Haley tucked her book into her bag and stood up. "I suppose so." She shook her head. "Don't you find it wonderful that we've all found men that are impervious to Savannah Douglas?"

"Yes, just wonderful," Alex said, sighing.

As Haley walked across the street, she thought she saw Savannah dig her claws further into Wes's skin. She would have laughed had the woman not been damaging her man.

"There you are. I thought you'd gotten lost." Haley walked over and stopped right next to Wes. She could see the relief in his eyes and smiled a little when he bent down and placed a kiss on her lips.

"Sorry, just had to drop that paperwork off at the bank," he mumbled.

"Yes, isn't it wonderful?" Savannah piped in. "Our Wes is going to be a property owner." She playfully slapped his arm, while still hanging onto it. "I was just trying to persuade him to take me for a drive and show me the place."

Haley's back teeth clenched together. Is that why he had needed to go to the bank? She had assumed he needed to make a deposit or withdraw. Now, she had to find out that he was actually going through with his plans and buying a place. From Savannah, no less!

She didn't know what to say. Her jaw refused to release so she just nodded and looked Wes in the eyes. She saw him pleading at her, but after what he'd just kept from her, she could care less if he was stuck with Savannah for the next year.

"Yes," she said before she realized it. "You should take her there. After all, it's such a nice day for a drive."

Haley headed for her car. She didn't feel like waiting for Alex to get off shift anymore. She was halfway to her car when Wes caught up with her and took her arm.

"Haley, what was that all about?" He stopped her and frowned down at her.

"What?" She pushed his hand off her arm.

"That." He motioned to where Savannah was standing at the corner, looking at them and pouting.

"Oh, I just thought that since the two of you had such a wonderful secret together, that you would want to share it together." She turned to walk away.

"Haley, listen, I told you--" he started.

She shook her head, interrupting him. "No, I'm done listening. I don't care if you spend your days or evenings with her." She nodded to where Savannah stood, her arms crossed over her chest as she waited for Wes. "But I won't be the last to know what's going on with you anymore. If you cared enough"—her voice lost some of its pitch as she felt the headache building— "you would be the one to tell me, first." She opened her car door, then looked over her shoulder. "Don't worry about coming over tonight."

She knew it was childish, but it felt so good to slam the door and drive away.

When she arrived home, she rushed into the house, but instead of heading up to her room she found herself at the bottom of the attic stairs. She felt her heart beating hard as she took the stairs slowly. She didn't know what sent her up there, but something called her to an old chest she had filled with some of her childhood memories.

When she sat down on the dusty floor, the shoebox of Wes's things on her lap, she could feel the tears rolling down her cheeks. Blinking them away, she lifted the lid and saw an image of them at prom.

She took almost an hour looking through the memories; old dried flowers he'd given her, little love notes she'd read over and over again, a small stuffed frog he'd won at the fair. The memories were almost painful when she thought about the new game they were playing.

Then, at the bottom of the stack was a small drawing done in colored ink. She remembered that it was from art class in grade school. One of the first notes he'd ever given her. The child-like handwriting was big and a little faded.

"I like you. Do you like me?" There were the standard checkboxes with yes and no beside them.

She'd marked back in purple ink, yes. Followed by a few hearts.

Closing her eyes, she remembered seeing his smile from across the room, when he'd read that note. That was the moment she'd lost her heart to him.

She knew she was fighting a losing battle. Hell, she'd lost it that day long ago, in art class. Why was she even trying anymore?

Taking the box with her, she walked back downstairs and into her room. When she set the box down on her desk, she looked at herself in the mirror and tried to figure out why it mattered so much that they pick up where they left off.

Flinging herself on the bed, she stared at her ceiling. So he was buying a place. She didn't know exactly where, or when it was going to happen, but she was almost certain that Savannah did. Flipping over, she crossed her arms in front of her and stared out the window. What other secrets did he keep from her?

She'd hoped to know what he planned for the future, but she'd wanted him to tell her, wanted him to share it with her. She'd never expected to learn them from Savannah. It only made it all so much more terrible.

She must have cried herself to sleep because the sound of someone knocking on her door jolted her.

"Yes?" She sat up as Lauren walked in. Her silver dress clung to her curves, her long hair piled up on the top of her head. Curls hung around her sister's face.

"Oh, don't you look wonderful." She scooted to the end of the bed.

"What's wrong?" Lauren walked over and sat next to her.

Shaking her head, she smiled. "Nothing, just one of those days." She patted her sister's hand, not wanting to spoil their special night. "Go. Have a great night in Tyler."

"Are you sure? We could—"

"Don't you dare. You've had these concert tickets for two months. Go celebrate. You deserve it."

Lauren smiled and then squealed. "Okay." She jumped up and spun around. "Can you believe we're having another baby?"

Haley smiled as she stood and hugged her sister. "I bet this time it's a girl. I just know it."

"Oh, I hope you're right." Lauren hugged her back. "Well, we better go. Ricky is downstairs, waiting for his play date with one of his favorite aunts."

"One? I am his favorite." They laughed.

An hour later, after playing cars with Ricky, she walked into the kitchen to make PB&Js. Ricky was on her hip and she almost screamed when she saw Wes standing outside the glass doors, ready to knock.

"Sorry," he said through the glass. "Can I come in?"

She was about to say no when Ricky chimed in, "Wessss, Wessss," and held his arms out towards the glass.

Caving to the two-year-old, she walked over and flipped open the door.

"Evening." He smiled and held out his arms for Ricky to jump into. "There's my little man."

"Wesss." Ricky grabbed his face and forced him to look at him. "Peanut butter, jelly." The little boy pointed to Haley.

"Yes, I'll stay for some peanut butter and jelly sandwiches," Wes said, smiling over the little boy's dark head at her.

They sat in the living room, a large blanket spread out on the floor, as they watched Scooby and ate PB&J.

Wes looked so funny sitting cross-legged, balancing a paper plate with a sandwich on his knee.

For his part, Ricky had jelly and peanut butter all over his face and fingers. Every time he touched her or Wes, they ended up messier than he was.

By the time the DVD of Scooby was over, Ricky's plate was empty, and the little boy's head was drooping.

"Come on, little guy. Time for your bath."

"Baff." Ricky jumped up and started running towards the stairs.

"Hang on!" She hurried after him, laughing.

When the water was ready, Haley lowered Ricky into the tub with all his favorite animal toys. Wes stood leaning against the bathroom sink, his arms and ankles crossed as he laughed and watched her play with her nephew.

By the time she pulled Ricky out of the water, she was completely soaked. She helped him put on his Superman pajamas, then he started jumping on his bed, screaming.

"Story, story."

"Why don't you go change into something dry. I can

read Superman his bedtime story," Wes said, walking over to Ricky's bookcase. Ricky jumped off his bed and rushed over.

"This one." He pulled out his favorite book, one Haley had read to him at least a hundred times.

"Are you sure?" She looked between the two.

He laughed and nodded. "I can read, you know."

She crossed her arms and glared at him.

"Story, Wesss," Ricky said, tugging on his hand as he carried the oversized book to his bed.

"Okay, I'll be just a minute." She turned and left the room.

She walked into her room, closed her door, and leaned back against it. Closing her eyes, she tried to block out how Wes had looked playing with Ricky, how great he'd been with her nephew.

Why was he doing this to her? Couldn't he see that he was making her miserable? She wanted to be with him, forever. But every time she stepped closer, he threw something else at her that shook her belief that he wanted her.

She needed to feel like she could trust him. Like he wasn't hiding anything from her. She knew there was still so much he was keeping from her.

Chase was right; they couldn't go back to how they used to be. They used to trust each other completely. They used to be able to tell each other anything. Now she didn't know if he still felt the same way about her.

Sure, he'd said he loved her, but he'd been on some serious pain pills at the time. Walking over to her closet, she yanked off the wet clothes and pulled on a clean pair of yellow yoga pants and an oversized white T-shirt. Comfort clothes.

Pulling her soaked hair up into a ponytail, she brushed her teeth, trying to convince herself that she was not going to make out with Wes on the couch until Lauren and Chase arrived home.

When she walked down the hall and looked into Ricky's room, she couldn't help smiling.

Ricky was fast asleep as Wes read the story in a warm, rich voice. She walked up behind him and laid her hand on his shoulder. When he looked up at her, she nodded, and he followed her out of the room.

"He falls asleep fast." She smiled as she shut the door.

"I think he was out after I read the title." Wes laughed. "Oh, to have the ability to fall asleep that fast, again." He shook his head and took her hand.

"Would you like some popcorn and an old movie?" she blurted out, feeling nervous.

He smiled slowly. "I'd love some popcorn and an old movie."

Wes sat on the couch and listened as Haley made the popcorn. She refused his help but did allow him to carry in two glasses of ice and some Cokes, and she allowed him to pick the movie out.

He was flipping through the DVDs and stopped when he came to her favorite movie. He knew she'd seen it a million times and knew all the words by heart, but still, he dropped it in the player and cued it up.

"Here we are," she said a few minutes later. She had a large silver bowl in her hands. The popcorn was piled high and covered with salt and butter, just the way they both liked it. "What movie did you pick out?" She set the bowl down and sat next to him.

"Grease." He smiled when she smiled back at him.

"Perfect." She took a sip of her Coke as he started the movie.

By the time the credit song was over, he'd moved her closer. They sat huddled, sharing the large bowl of popcorn, and by the end of the first song, his arm was around her. A few minutes later, he pulled her into his lap as he kissed her breathless.

He'd missed her. Her taste. The feel of her. She was like a drug that he couldn't live without. He'd let his hair grow a little more, so when she pushed her fingers through it, he heard her groan.

She leaned back and readjusted so that she was straddling him now, her hands on his chest. His hands rested comfortably on her hips.

"Why didn't you tell me you were buying a place?" she asked, looking down at him. He could see her eyes showed the hurt.

He shrugged his shoulders and looked up at her. "I did, remember?" When she shook her head, no, he continued, "Besides, I had hoped it would be a surprise."

Closing his eyes, he tried to block out his hunger, knowing that she wanted to talk now instead of continuing with their make-out session.

"Why?" she asked. When he opened his eyes, he saw her frowning a little.

He pulled her down closer until they looked eye to eye. "Haley, I want to be with you. You've known that since the second grade." He smiled.

She shook her head. "I just don't . . ." She started to pull back.

"No, please." He groaned when she brushed up against his desire. He watched her eyes get bigger with surprise and thought he saw heat there as well. "Don't pull away from me. I'm trying to readjust to being home." He shook his head.

"I'm sorry, I didn't think about how difficult it must be for you."

He ran his hand up her back and watched her reaction. "I didn't have a nightmare last night."

She smiled and tilted her head a little. "Really? That's good news."

He nodded. "I dreamed of our children. Of the place, I'm hoping to buy on Bond Drive. Of our family." He cupped her face. "I wanted it so bad, I forgot to clue you in on my plans." He smiled but watched her face drop a little. "What? Don't you like the old place?"

She shook her head. "It's not that."

"Because I'm having a new double-wide moved there as soon as the bank approves me."

She smiled. "It's not the house. I just . . ."

"What?"

She closed her eyes and sighed. "I feel like there is this wedge." She motioned between them. "Do you understand?"

He shook his head.

"There's something you're not telling me, a part of you that you've been holding back. I've felt it ever since you got home."

He shook his head again. "I don't understand."

She sighed and closed her eyes. "Maybe it's all in my

head." When she opened her eyes again, she ran her fingers through his hair. "I like that you've grown it longer again."

He smiled and pulled her closer until he could feel her breath on his face. When she bent down to kiss him, his hands shook her hips. The coarse material of his jeans did little to hide the fact that he wanted her. As she kissed him, her hips moved slowly over his bulge, until he wondered if she would cause him to come in his pants without even touching him.

"Haley," he pulled away a little.

"No, just a little more." She moaned, and he could see that she was on the verge.

Moving her down underneath him, he pushed her legs wider and rested between her, core to core. Her head rolled back and her eyes slid closed.

Slowly he moved his hands until his fingers felt under the elastic and found her moist and hot for him. Using his fingertips, he pinched her sensitive skin until she purred and moaned, her hips moving with his fingers, which were growing slick from her desire. He wanted to pull down her pants and quickly embed himself, but he knew it wasn't the time or place.

Dipping his head, he took her nipple into his mouth through her white T-shirt. He sucked until he felt the bud pucker. Then he pushed two fingers quickly into her heat, causing her nails to dig into his shoulders as she gasped.

"More," he growled as he watched her face. Her cheeks were flushed, and her lips were swollen from his kisses. "More, give me more."

She shook her head, keeping her eyes closed tightly. "I can't," she moaned. "Too much," she said as her hips rose and fell with each thrust of his hand. "Please," she begged just before he felt the slickness of her release.

He kissed her until he felt her relax in his arms. "You're so beautiful when you come." He smiled down at her.

She opened her eyes and smiled at him. "Really?"

He nodded. "You glow."

She reached up and punched his shoulder lightly. "You're delusional."

He shook his head from side to side. "When can you come over again?" He moved until they lay side by side as the movie played.

"Hmm, tomorrow. No, wait. I'm going to Tyler with Alex tomorrow. Aunties need to go on a shopping spree for the new baby." She smiled and looked back at him. "It's sort of our tradition."

"What about coming over after?"

She nodded. "Sounds like a plan."

"I'd like to drive you up to the place on Bond. If you want to see it."

She nodded. "I'd like that." Then she laughed. "How did you get out of driving Savannah up there today?"

He frowned. "I told her I had another meeting. That woman has never shown interest in me before. I don't get why she is now."

"Because she can, and she's desperate. Ever since Travis left town, she hasn't had a steady bang," she said, then let out a large yawn.

He let her watch the TV for a while as he rubbed his fingers up and down her arm.

When she was fast asleep, he lay there and dreamed of his new life with her.

Haley woke when she heard Lauren and Chase come home. Wes was fast asleep behind her, his leg pinning her to the cushions. Haley saw the surprise on her sister's face, then the slow smile that spread. Lauren quickly walked backward out of the room, giving her two thumbs up as she went.

Haley tried not to laugh, but it was just too funny. She felt Wes stir behind her and snuggled back down for the night on a lumpy couch and in the arms of a man she was desperately trying not to love too much.

By morning, she wondered why she hadn't just moved them up to her bedroom. Her neck was at an odd angle and her right hip was off the couch. Wes's arms were still wrapped around her tightly, but even so, she was slipping off the couch and soon would be on the floor.

"Mmmm," Wes said, as he buried his face into her hair. "What a wonderful way to wake up." His hands started roaming over her, pulling her closer so she was lying over him now. She moved until she was facing him and started raining kisses over his face and neck.

He felt too good not to touch, and she reached up under his shirt and felt his heated skin with her fingertips. He moaned, and she could feel that he was totally aroused, which sent shivers down her body in anticipation.

Then they were attacked by a flying, dark-haired, two-year-old.

"Wessss, Wesss." Ricky jumped on her back, causing her breath to whoosh out quickly.

"Sorry," Lauren said from the door, laughing. "He escaped before I could grab him." She smiled and pulled her robe closer around her waist.

Haley laughed as Ricky sat on her butt and started riding her like a pony, her long braid in his hands.

"Get up, Haley. Get up."

Wes laughed.

"Come on, Ricky, let's go get you some cereal," Lauren said, trying to encourage her son to leave the room.

"Wesss eat cereal too?"

"Sure, I'll be right in." When Ricky jumped off Haley's back and raced from the room, she looked down at Wes with a smile.

"Sorry, I should have known we wouldn't have time alone. Not with a two-year-old in the house."

"That's okay, I don't mind Ricky. He's my Roger." He smiled up at her.

"No nightmares last night?" She realized he hadn't woken her up.

He shook his head. "You've cured me." He smiled at her again.

After eating some Cocoa Puffs, toast, and orange juice, Wes headed back to his place. Haley promised she'd be by later that day, so they could drive up to the place on Bond and then go back to his place for dinner.

After he left, she showered and made her daily rounds. She had been working with the calf, Roger. Since spotting how intelligent he was, she'd moved him to the smaller corral with his mother. The boy had a way about him. He constantly made her laugh, and she found herself falling head over heels for the little guy. He wasn't the best looking or the fastest, but he was smart, and his coat was well taken care of, thanks to all her hard work.

She ended up spending more time with him than some of her other animals.

Blackjack, her five-year-old, blue-ribbon California Gray rooster, who never stayed in his pen, had always followed her around. But since he'd made friends with Roger, the rooster was never far from Roger's side. The two of them actually played tag. Well, what she thought of as tag.

Roger would lean down and tip his nose to Blackjack's tail feathers. Then Blackjack would take off running, with Roger right behind. It was funny to watch when the tables turned, and Blackjack chased the hundred-pound calf around the yard, as was going on currently. She sat on the top rung of the fence and chuckled at the sight.

"You've got a real winner there." Chase laughed as he leaned on the post next to her.

"They do make an odd couple."

"Speaking of couples." He tilted his hat back and looked at her.

She sighed, then looked off at the game, not really noticing it anymore. "I don't know yet. He's taking me to see the land he's trying to buy. He says he wants me to be a part of his future, but . . ." She shook her head. "He's not the same person. I feel like I stood still, and he . . ."

Chase patted her knee. "Haley, he's still Wes. I didn't know him all that well since you guys are a lot younger, but everyone in town can see it. He still has it bad for you. And," he smiled and tipped his hat back, shading his eyes, "if I'm not mistaken, you still have it bad for him."

Her smile faltered a little. She did still have it bad for

him. If she had just gone with her gut instincts, she would have welcomed him back with open arms. But her heart still hurt when she thought about everything he was still keeping from her.

Chase broke her thoughts when he cussed under his breath. "If that woman doesn't kill herself, I'm fixin' to do it for her." He marched off towards the barn where Lauren was busy trying to get on the back of a horse.

Haley chuckled and watched Chase grab his wife gently by the hips and hold her still as he talked quietly to her. Lauren put her hands on her hips for a minute, then nodded as they started walking towards the house together, leaving the horse standing in the shade of the barn.

She knew her sister was stubborn. Hell, it ran in the West family. Lauren had run this place all by herself for almost ten years. She thought her sister thought of herself as indestructible. Alex had been engaged to the wrong man for almost that same amount of time until Grant had come along and rescued her from a big mistake.

Maybe she was falling into the same pattern that her sisters had. Both of them had fought love when it had come to them. They had needed a little push in order for everything to end up the way it had. Maybe she wasn't giving love a chance.

Determined not to be a fool, she finished her chores and went inside to get ready for her date.

By the time she walked out the front door in one of her summer dresses, the clouds had rolled in and it had started raining lightly. She always dreaded summer weather. She enjoyed it when it rained since it always made everything so green and smell so fresh, but she hated the lightning and thunder that usually came with it.

Jogging towards her car, she shivered when the fat drops landed on her shoulders. It was still in the high eighties, but the water felt cold on her skin.

She drove down the road and in less than a minute, she pulled up beside his truck. He stood on the covered front porch, smiling at her. When she opened her door, he was there with an umbrella, shielding her from the heavy rain that was now pelting down on them.

"So much for a quiet drive tonight," he shouted over the loud downpour.

She smiled as he shook off the umbrella. "I don't mind. We needed the rain."

"Yes, I suppose so. Well, what do you say to dinner first, then if this clears up, a drive later?"

"Sounds good." She walked into his arms and kissed him slowly.

"Mmm, maybe dinner later," he said, walking her backward through the door.

She chuckled when her back came up against the door instead.

"Sorry," he grumbled, then smiled. "I'm usually smoother than this." His hands were running down her sides. "Have I told you how beautiful you look?"

The heat in his eyes caused her breath to hitch. Shaking her head, she gasped when he dipped his head and nibbled on her ear.

She moaned when he whispered next to her neck, "So beautiful, you taste like spring." He pushed open the door and walked her backward until her knees hit the side of his bed. Then he stood back and looked down at her.

"I've wanted you since the last time. So much. Too

much." His hands went up and cupped her face and she could see the desire in his dark eyes that matched her own.

"Wes?" She couldn't explain what he was doing to her. For so long she'd imagined being with him like this again. Going slow as the rain pelted down on the metal roof overhead. Making love until the sunset and the stars came out.

"Haley." He pulled back and looked at her again. "I want to make love to you. Let me show you." His fingers shook as he used just his fingertips to lower the shoulders of her dress, exposing her skin for his lips to brush over. "You're so soft, so smooth." His fingers pushed her dress down farther as his lips left a burning trail over her shoulders.

Her head fell back as her fingers went into his hair, holding him, guiding him. "Please," she moaned, wanting more.

A flash of lightning lit up the dim room, causing her to jolt.

"Still afraid of thunder?" he asked, coming back to kiss her lips. She nodded her head and jolted as the thunder crashed close by.

"Focus on me, then. On what I'm doing to you." He'd known her weakness for the weather, had always known why she didn't like the thunder.

She tried to focus on the feel of him touching her, kissing her, instead of the dread that was building up behind her heart. When his hands cupped her bare breasts, she realized her mind had wandered to that dreadful day so many years ago. Then his lips and tongue played over her nipples and she forgot all about the weather.

Gasping, she held onto his hair as he lapped at her

skin. He sucked lightly on her nipples and she felt herself go wet. How did he have such power over her?

"You taste like honey," he moaned as he knelt in front of her. Gently pushing her sundress down farther, he smiled when he saw the lacy panties she wore underneath. "For me?" He looked up at her. When she nodded, he smiled. "Mmmm, I like them." He ran his fingertips over the lace, rubbing the soft material against her heated skin.

She felt the panties go wet from her desire and moaned when he bent his head and tasted her through the light material. When he had soaked the white material, he pushed it to the side and ran his tongue over her naked skin, lapping at her until she felt her knees go weak. Then he nudged her until she sat at the edge of the bed.

Not wanting to lose all control, she pulled him down with her. He smiled when she kicked off the dress and pressed his shoulders to the mattress.

"My turn." She smiled down at him. Her fingers were steady as she pulled open the buttons of his shirt. He helped her pull his shirts off, but she pushed him back to the mattress when he started reaching for her. "No, still my turn." She smiled down at him.

Dipping her head, she ran her mouth and tongue over his chest. He'd been a boy, really, when she'd last explored him like this. Now his chest was wider and full of new muscles, which she took time to explore. Her fingers traveled down his six-pack and played with the light trail of hair that traveled from his navel to below his jeans. When she reached for his belt, his fingers dug into the comforter next to him. "Haley, you're killing me," he said between clenched teeth.

"Good. Enjoy it. I know I am." She flipped open his

belt and jeans, then lightly tugged on them until they were sitting below his hips with his boxers. His erection sprang out and she moaned. He was so beautiful. She'd never seen another man, but she doubted they would compare to Wes. His skin was soft, yet he was hard as stone. Dipping her head, she ran her mouth down his happy trail and then licked the head of his erection. He jumped as his hands went into her hair.

"Please," he groaned as she took him all the way into her mouth.

She had never enjoyed herself more as she used her mouth to bring him to the edge like he'd done to her.

His legs were still trapped in his jeans and boxers, so when he moved to push her underneath him, he had to stand as she waited, trying not to burst herself.

When he was freed of his boots and jeans, he flipped her onto the bed with a laugh. "Now you're going to get it." He smiled down at her. But instead of coming down with her, he stood above her and just looked at her.

Her hands went to her breasts, pushing them together as she watched his eyes heat. "Yes, touch yourself," he said, watching her every move.

Her hands roamed down her sides until she touched where his eyes burned her. She saw him moan and reach for a condom from his nightstand. After shielding himself, he knelt between her legs.

"Yes, keep touching yourself," he said, as he positioned himself at her entrance. "Does that feel good?" he asked as he started to slide in.

Her head fell back, and her hand fell away as he moved above her. Then he was moving inside her and kissing her until she couldn't control the scream of release.

Wes lay there and listened to the storm building. Thunderstorms were a common thing in the area, and he knew that the stream behind the row of houses could easily grow to three times its normal size. He had an app on his phone that alerted him to such storms, but he didn't want to move just yet.

Haley's and his breathing had finally returned to normal, and their bodies had cooled in the night air. The lightning and thunder were still raging outside, and he was happy that she was still too dazed to realize it.

He knew why she hated the bad weather. It all went back to when her mother had died in a tornado when she was four.

Once, when they had been teenagers, they had met at the pond one summer and had been caught up in a storm. They had sought shelter in an old cattle barn on her property. He'd never seen someone have a panic attack like she'd had that day. He was sure that if he hadn't been there, she would have died of fright. He'd done his best to calm her, but he was relieved when her father had shown up shortly after the storm had ended to take her home.

Just then the house shook with thunder and she bolted up.

"Hey." He reached for her, but he could tell that she was already too far gone to help. Her eyes were huge, her skin was pasty and pale. She was shaking and when he wrapped a blanket around her, her teeth started chattering.

"Haley." He took her face in his hands. "Focus on me, baby. I'm here. We're safe."

She shook her head.

"Damn it." He jumped from the bed and grabbed one of his large sweatshirts and pulled it over her head. "Here," he tried to pull her hands through the sleeves. He knew she was freezing and wanted to get her warm. When she didn't push her arms through, he thought of a different tactic and pulled the sweatshirt off her again.

Picking her up, he carried her towards the bathroom. Setting her on the countertop, he started the shower and pushed the heat to full. When the water was steaming, he carried her right into the shower and set her down under the spray.

She shivered for a few moments until he started running his hands over her hair, her shoulders. He felt her starting to relax, muscle by muscle.

"Easy," he murmured softly to her, continuing to tell her how beautiful she was, how much he loved her until he felt her completely relax in his arms. When he ran his hands over her hips, over her breasts, he felt her tense again, this time with desire.

"Wes," she moaned as he ran his mouth over her wet skin.

"I want you. I can't stop wanting you," he said against her skin. She was like a drug. Her skin was addictive, her taste intoxicating. He wanted to feel her wrapped around him, body and soul.

"I want you, too." Her hands began running over him, causing his skin to heat even more. "I missed this for years. I missed you."

He leaned her back against the shower wall and helped her prop her leg up on the side of the bathtub. "We might end up killing ourselves, but I don't care." He chuckled. "Hang onto me, baby," he said as he slid into her slowly.

Twin moans filled the room, drowning out the sound of the now-distant thunder.

When he started to move, her nails dug into his sides and her eyes closed tightly. He'd never seen anything more beautiful in his life. Her hair was flowing around her breasts. Her green eyes opened slowly, reminding him of the waters in the Persian Gulf.

He lapped at her wet skin and used his hips to pin her to the side of the shower, not wanting to let her go. Their naked skin rubbed together, causing friction and heating the small room even more.

"Please," she begged, shaking her head and her hair back and forth. "Please, Wes."

"God!" he groaned, then reached down between them and touched her heat with a fingertip. He watched her explode just before he followed her.

By the time he carried her back to the bed, the storm had passed, and she relaxed in his bed as he made them cold turkey sandwiches. They lay there and ate a bag of potato chips as they watched a rerun of Gilligan's Island until they fell asleep in each other's arms. He dreamed, once again, about green-eyed, brown-haired children running through the fields, playing with animals as he and Haley sat and watched from the front porch.

CHAPTER 11

The following morning, they drove up to Bond Drive, just on the outskirts of the state park. The land was pretty with its large oak and pine trees. There were plenty of grassy fields where cows and horses could roam. Even the barn could be fixed up to accommodate animals.

The house, however, was a complete loss. There was a large tree branch through the living room roof. The front door was propped open by a large stone, and when they tried to walk in, Wes's foot fell through a small hole in the front porch. He laughed and pulled it out.

"Another reason this place will be bulldozed. The VA wouldn't approve my loan with it standing here." He shook his head. "It's a pity, too. I heard this place used to be really nice."

"I can only remember it like this," she said, jumping over another hole in the floorboards. The place smelled of mildew and animals.

"Well, like I said, I've picked out a double-wide that

the VA has approved. If all goes well after they approve my loan I can have this place torn down and that one moved up here shortly after." They stopped in the kitchen area, one of the only areas that still looked like the inside of a house instead of a scene from a horror movie.

"Haley?" He turned to her, taking both her hands in his. "I know it's not much to look at now, but soon it will be and . . ." He broke off as he turned a little pasty.

"Wes?" She began to worry and stepped closer to him. "Are you okay?"

He smiled and laughed a little. "Yes, it's just . . ." He shook his head. "Come outside with me. I want you to see the view."

She followed him in silence as they walked hand in hand to the middle of one of the fields. There were a few large oak trees, and when they reached the top of a small hill, she could see forever.

Gasping, she spun around to see the entire view. "How wonderful." She crossed her arms over her chest and hugged herself. "You can see forever. I never knew this place was here." She shook her head in disbelief. When she turned back towards Wes, he was on his knee holding up a small brown box.

"Haley Marie West, I've loved you since the second grade. You've been my best friend for as long as I can remember. I love you with all of my heart and want to spend the rest of my days with you here, on our land, raising kids and animals. Please marry me."

She stood there, looking down at him and not knowing what to say. So many things went through her head at that moment. So many questions.

Could she take it if he broke her heart again? Would

he? She shook her head, answering her own question, and saw the color leave his face.

"No," she said quickly. "It's not . . ." She bent down next to him, the knee of her jeans getting soaked with the wet grass and ground. "Wes." She grabbed his face and forced him to look at her. "I have wanted nothing more than to be married to you for as long as I can remember."

She watched the color flood back into his face. His eyes started to shine, and he smiled at her.

"Then say yes." He held up the box again.

She couldn't say it, so instead just nodded her head. He let out a happy cry and lifted her and spun her in circles.

By the time they drove back to Saddleback Ranch and told everyone the news, she was beyond tired. Her sisters had never looked happier than when they told them the news. Chase and Grant had shaken Wes's hand and welcomed him to the family.

Wes had ended up staying around for the rest of the day, helping the men fix a gate that was giving them some problems. She had spent most of her day taking care of her animals and timing Alex for her barrel racing.

After dinner, they sat out on the back deck, watching the sunset. The sun and heat had returned, making the evening muggy.

The bugs and frogs were buzzing tonight, the sounds drowning out almost everything else as they swung slowly.

"You know; I was thinking about it . . ." he began.

"Uh-oh," she interrupted, causing him to laugh.

"No, seriously, why don't you move in with me at the ranch house? I know it's small, but we can get a head start on living like a real couple." He held her hand and brought it to his lips.

She shook her head. "Oh, no. You don't get out of it that easy." She smiled. "The West sisters know how to throw a big wedding. There is no sneaking off to Vegas and getting married for us."

He looked innocent. "That's not what I had in mind, really." He smiled. "Well, maybe."

She smiled at him. "Wesley Aaron Tanner, I know you too well." He cringed when she called him by his full name. She knew he hated it, and she had only called him that one other time before.

"Okay, okay." He smiled. "I'll behave. How about an October wedding?"

She laughed. "I need more than a month to get everything ready."

He smiled and nodded. "November it is then."

She laughed and realized she wasn't as tired as she had initially thought.

"I was thinking of getting a couple dogs." He looked over at her. "You know, for when the house is all settled and everything.

"That sounds like a plan." She leaned back against his shoulder and sighed.

"I'd hoped that kids would follow shortly after."

She sat up a little and turned to him. "Kids?"

He nodded. "I know you doubted me when I said that I was really looking forward to having kids. Even back then."

She shook her head. Emotions flooded too deep. "I—I don't."

He took her face in his hands, "Haley, I've dreamed about our kids every night since the nightmares have stopped. It's the one thing that keeps me grounded to here, now."

"This isn't real," she said, her breath hitching.

He leaned forward and kissed her lips, wet with tears. "It's real."

Wes was on cloud nine. For the next few days, he jumped through every hoop the bank asked and did everything to make sure the VA had their part taken care of. The loan for the trailer was secure, as long as he had land to place it on.

It drove him nuts having his future up in the air like this. He wished he had the money to buy everything outright, but as it was, his checks from the army were barely going to cover his loans. He knew he had to find a job but wasn't sure what it was that he wanted to do. The military had taken a lot from him, and he knew he still needed time to recoup it all.

He was standing in the bank line once again with the paperwork they needed to guarantee his loan when the door burst open and a shot rang out. It was more instinct than anything, but he hit the floor, taking Mrs. Wilkins, one of his old high school teachers, down with him. Shielding her body with his, he watched as three masked men walked into the bank, armed to the teeth.

"On the floor—now!" the largest of the group said with a thick accent. Wes's years of training kicked in and he noticed everything about the men, down to the fact that they all wore work boots covered in red clay.

"Not you," the thinner man said, pointing his gun at Steve, who was trying to crouch behind the counter. Steve stood back up, his arms up in the air. "Empty it." He pointed the gun towards Steve's drawer, then tossed a black duffel back through the opening in the glass.

Wes watched the other two men as the thin one waited for Steve. The silent one stood by the door watching the street while the big one paced around the room, eager.

"Come on," he said, several times. "Hurry."

Wes knew what he needed to do. He'd been trained just for situations like this. Sometimes you fought, sometimes you ran, other times you remembered everything you could and stayed out of the way of flying bullets. These men were professionals. He would stake his life that this wasn't their first rodeo. They worked great as a team and he was sure they had worked together in another job.

Then it came to him. Down on Highway 59, there was a large construction crew building the new highway in Redland. It was the only place with red clay for miles around. Looking at their work boots again, he noticed a yellow triangle sticker on the big man's boots. Gotcha, he thought as he tried to hush Mrs. Welkins.

"Keep that bitch quiet," the big man said, bringing his boot up to kick at them. Wes turned just in time to catch the boot on his thigh. Pain shot up and down his hurt leg and he grunted.

"Leave him alone. You promised no one would be hurt this time," the man at the door said. Wes noticed the lack of accent in his voice and the fact that he held the gun with his left hand.

"It's full," the thin man said, rushing to the door. "Are we clear?"

When lefty nodded, the three of them bolted from the building. Wes rushed to the door just in time to see them disappear around the corner of Bridles Books, the local bookstore right next to Mama's.

He looked at Steve, who was still standing behind the counter, his arms up in the air. "Call the sheriff," he yelled, just before he rushed out of the front door, his leg screaming at him as he hobbled towards the bookstore.

He made it around the corner to see a white Ford F150 peel out of the parking lot.

"Damn," he said when he couldn't read the plates. The truck was too far away for him to even tell if they were Texas plates. But he did see the red dirt all over the back tailgate.

By the time he walked back to the bank, the sheriff was just pulling in. "Wes." He rushed over to him. "Are you okay, son?"

He realized then that he was limping more than before. "Damn," he said. "Yes, the bastard kicked me in the leg."

"Come on inside and sit down while you tell me what happened." The sheriff helped him walk into the glass doors, where Mrs. Wilkins was crying into Steve's arms. Steve looked pale and even Betty was crying gently in a chair. When she saw him limp in, she quickly rushed to his side.

"Are you okay, Wes?" She helped him sit in the chair. "Do you need some ice?"

He shook his head. "If someone would call Haley and let her know that I'll need a ride home, that would be great."

He knew he'd done some more damage to his leg. He didn't need a Ph.D. to realize something wasn't right after the steel-toed boot had made its mark on his thigh.

"I can drive you to the clinic," Betty said, looking concerned.

He shook his head. "No, I'll be fine. I'm seeing a doctor at the VA tomorrow." He rubbed his thigh and cringed when pain shot up to his chest.

"Wes?" The sheriff stood over him and grabbed his shoulders. "Betty, get him some water."

He bent over and took several deep breaths. "Work boots. White Ford 150. Red mud. Two spoke with Georgia accents. Big man, skinny kid. Lefty didn't speak with an accent." He blurted out the details, trying to stay conscious. The pain was almost unbearable. "Big man had yellow hazmat sticker on his work boots. They work together; most likely they've done this before." He took several deep breaths and felt himself whiting out. Then he heard her voice.

"Wes?" She rushed to his side. "I'm here."

His mind sharpened as he felt her hands on his face. Looking up, he smiled at her. "There you are," he said, just before passing out.

CHAPTER 12

The doctors wouldn't tell her anything. She paced up and down the halls of the VA hospital in Tyler, wanting to rip someone's tongue out. When she asked about him, all they kept telling her was, "He's in surgery." She knew he was in surgery. What she didn't know was why.

Betty had told the paramedics that one of the robbers had kicked him in his left leg, hard, right where he'd had the blood vessel replacement.

Had the kick caused it to rupture? Were they having to redo the surgery?

Her family was sitting in the waiting room with Wes's family and half the town of Fairplay. Everyone but Haley was patiently waiting for news in the small room. She was pacing just outside the operating room doors, ready to jump when the doors opened.

She'd never bitten her nails as a child—Alex was the one who'd chewed her fingers down to the bone—but now, she was nibbling on them like they were candy.

Just then, the doors swung open and the doctor, an older man, walked out and pulled down his surgical mask so he could talk to her.

"Mrs. Tanner?" she nodded, without saying a word. She felt his parents rush to her side; her mother took her hand in hers.

"He's out of surgery. The kick to his leg damaged his blood vessel. There was massive internal bleeding, but we stopped it quickly enough. We had to do an emergency peripheral artery bypass." When the three of him just looked at him, he shook his head. "Sorry, we had to replace the section of vein that was damaged from before. Basically, the last time, we had grafted a blood vessel from his right leg. This time we had to use a plastic tube since the vein was damaged. He'll need to stay in ICU for a few days. Then we'll move him to a private room for a week or so, just to watch him. He'll need to stay off that leg for a while."

She nodded. "When can I see him?"

"In about an hour." He patted her hand. "I'll have a nurse come get you. They only allow one visitor at a time, though, and they close at eight."

They all nodded. She knew she wouldn't relax until she saw him for herself. When they had loaded him into the ambulance, he'd been white as a sheet and unconscious. She'd wanted to ride with him but had been denied. Instead, Grant had driven her and Alex behind the ambulance. Thankfully, Grant had been at Mama's picking up Alex after her shift.

His parents guided her back into the waiting room. She felt numb. She sat down on a couch next to her sister and sipped the coffee someone shoved into her hands. She could vaguely hear as his parents passed on the news to everyone who'd been waiting.

An hour later, a young nurse walked in and showed her into the ICU. He was unconscious and still so very pale. His dark hair and eyelashes looked even darker against his light skin. When she reached for his hand, she noticed all the tubes sticking out and walked over to take his other hand, which was clear. She leaned over and placed a kiss on his cool lips. Tears were streaming down her face, and when she leaned forward, they fell onto his skin.

Using shaking fingers, she wiped them off his almost translucent skin. "Wes?" she said, not sure if he was awake or not. When his eyelids fluttered, she said his name again.

When his eyes opened all the way, she could tell that they were unfocused and foggy. "I'm here," she said, holding his hand tighter. "You're okay. Everything is going to be just fine," she repeated over and over as his eyelids slid closed again.

She sat with him until the nurse asked if his mother could take her place. She nodded and walked back into the waiting room and right into her sisters' arms.

"Sheriff Miller is here," Lauren said when she pulled back, nodding towards the older man who was standing against the wall talking to Betty and Steve.

He nodded at her and walked up to give her a hug. "How's he doing?"

"He's in and out. Did you catch the robbers?"

The sheriff nodded. "Thanks to Wes." He shook his head. "That boy has a talent for details. Knew everything about the men, down to their boots." He walked her over to the couch and they sat down together. "They worked on the road crew that's building the highway." He shook his head. "Wasn't their first job together either. Looks like they were the three robbers that killed that bank clerk in Alabama last spring. We have enough on them." He nodded to Steve and Betty, who was still sitting across the room with Mrs. Wilkins. "They've ID'd them. All it took was hearing the men speak." He shook his head again. "Don't rob a bank in a small town in Texas. They're lucky Wes jumped on Mrs. Wilkins."

Her eyebrows shot up in question.

"Mrs. Wilkins is a card-carrying member of the NRA." He laughed. "You wouldn't think of it to look at her"—he nodded toward the frail old woman across the room— "but she packs a .44 Magnum in that big purse of hers. I've seen her shoot a can off the fence from thirty yards." He laughed. "If Wes hadn't held her down, I'm afraid she would have gone all Rambo on us."

She smiled slightly, knowing the sheriff was trying to lighten her mood. A few minutes later, while she talked to Mrs. Wilkins, she realized it had worked. Seeing how many people cared about Wes and about her state of mind made her realize what a great town they lived in.

The next few days were a blur. She was in and out of the ICU every chance she could get. She split her time with the Tanners, who had always treated her like their daughter. When they moved him to a private room, she sat next to him as other people came and went. When they tried to kick her out for the night, she talked to the doctor and persuaded him to let her stay.

Wes was still going in and out of consciousness. He would gain his wits, but the pain was too much and the nurses would give him another pill, which would knock him out again. She begged them for medication that wouldn't make him loopy, but until most of his pain was bearable, their choices were limited.

On the fifth day after the bank robbery, Wes sat up in bed and threw the small cup full of pills across the room. The paper cup floated to the floor; the pills, however, scattered across the floor. The husky nurse put her hands on her hips and glared at him.

"No more. I'm done," he said softly, cringing a little.

The nurse just looked at him, then turned and left the room without a word. His doctor appeared less than ten minutes later.

"I hear you won't take any more pain pills," he said as he checked over his medical charts.

"That's right." Wes nodded, crossing his arms over his chest. "They make me loopy and besides, my pain is manageable now."

The doctor nodded. "That's good." He looked up from his charts. "How would you feel about starting physical therapy?"

Wes smiled and nodded. "Sounds great. I'm ready."

"Good, let's get you a cane."

Haley heard Wes groan and saw him roll his eyes as the doctor laughed. "I know you don't like canes but trust me"—he reached over and patted his hand— "this time you'll use it."

It took him almost three weeks to feel comfortable walking all by himself. His left thigh had been covered with dark bruises. Even his toes hurt on that leg, but he bore the pain and stayed off the pain pills. With the help of

Haley, he was walking with the use of a cane after the first week.

One positive thing came out of all this mess; he ended up getting his wish. Haley moved her stuff into his small house and stayed with him every night. She hardly left his side, usually only to take care of her animals and some chores.

His parents and half the town stopped by and visited. The sheriff had even stopped by and offered him a job, once he was back on his feet.

He'd been thinking about working in law since middle school. Now he knew he had the skills, and with just a little more school, he could even become a sheriff, himself. Of course, he'd have to start at a desk job first, until he was back to one hundred percent.

While he was in the hospital, he'd gotten word that his loan had been fully approved. Helping catch the robbers probably had something to do with pushing it through.

Haley had driven him down to the bank, and they'd put her name on the papers as well. The day they had closed on the land and house, he'd walked for the first time without his cane.

They headed over to Mama's to celebrate. When they walked in the doors, Wes was surprised that the small place was packed and decorated.

"Surprise!" everyone screamed as they walked in.

"What's this all about?" he asked Haley, who was smiling over at him.

She shook her head and pointed to the banner that read, "Congratulations to the new homeowners and the bank robber thwarter."

He laughed, then hugged his folks, then Jamella, then

half the town. He sat amongst his friends, listening to Steve retell the story of the robbery, and he laughed harder than he ever had. Steve could tell a great story, even if for most of the robbery, he'd been standing behind the counter, scared to death.

"You should have seen me shake," Steve said, taking another drink of his Coke. "I heard Jamella felt it and thought it was an earthquake." Everyone laughed. "You should have seen this one though." He held up his Coke and saluted Wes. "He hit the floor with Mrs. Wilkins faster than you could blink. Then he pushed her under him as that man tried to kick her. You know how fragile she is; her bones would have snapped under the pressure of those steel-toe boots. Those men might be facing murder charges by now if it wasn't for Wes."

Wes felt his cheeks flush and wished he had some fresh air. Haley squeezed his hand under the table and smiled at him. He knew he could do anything with her at his side.

Later that evening, she drove them back to their place in silence. When she pulled her car to a stop, she looked over at him, a smile no longer on her lips.

"What?" He took up her hand. "What's wrong?"

She shook her head. "It's nothing."

He looked at her, tilting his head, knowing better.

She chuckled. "Okay, it's just that after hearing the story from Steve, I realize how close it was."

He pulled her across the seat and hugged her. "Nothing can take me away from you." He pulled back, then kissed her gently. "Nothing. No power on Earth can stop me from being with you. Do you understand?"

She nodded and kissed him again. When the kiss

turned hot, he pulled back, knowing he was in no shape to have sex in the small car.

"Come on, let's get inside. It looks like rain again," he said, playfully pushing her off his lap.

They raced through the light rain until they reached the porch, where he pulled her closer to him and kissed her until he felt that the rain was steaming off his skin.

Just the feel of her skin against his lit fires all over his skin. He moved until she was up against the door as he ran his hands underneath her shirt. Her skin felt smooth and soft under his fingertips. She moaned when he pulled open her shirt and dipped his head to taste the exposed skin.

She fumbled for the door handle and pushed him inside, kicking the door shut with a quick motion. He had her pinned up against the door, quickly. Her hands were trapped above her wet hair, and her breathing was labored as she watched him with her sea-green eyes.

"You bewitch me," he said just before he took her mouth again. "Your skin is soft as flower petals." He ran his lips over her neck and shoulder, then pulled the shirt off until she was exposed. "You taste better than honey." He ran his tongue over the dip between her breasts. She moaned as he pushed her long skirt up her silky legs and up over her hips. When his fingers dipped under the silk that covered her, he groaned. "You feel better than heaven." He slid a finger into her heat and watched her eyes go dark.

"More," he groaned when her fingernails dug into his skin. "I want it all." He pushed her skirt higher, completely over her hips, and turned her around. Her hands came up, holding her away from the door as she flung her hips towards him.

He took hold of her hips after yanking his jeans down over his own hips. "Faster," she cried. "Now!"

He pushed her legs wider with his knees, then plunged into her in one quick motion. She cried out with pleasure as he pinned her to the door.

"Faster," she cried, throwing her head back.

His hips moved faster as he reached up with his hands and took hold of her breasts lightly.

"Please," she moaned. "More."

He turned her quickly, picking her up until she was pinned between him and the door. Her bare legs wrapped around his hips as he plunged into her deeper. Their mouths fused together. Their heartbeats and labored breaths matched.

"I want it all," he growled, not knowing what he was asking for.

Her fingers dug into his scalp as he thrust deeper and harder until finally, he felt her tighten around him. He felt her go completely lax against his body; only then did he find his own release.

That night, as Haley slept through the evening thunderstorm, he lay awake thinking of how close it had really been. He'd asked the doctors not to tell her how close he'd come. Hell, he hadn't known until a nurse had mentioned something about it.

When Haley started moaning and crying in her sleep, he pulled her near and ran his hands over her hair, cooing to her. She finally settled down as the storm passed and he fell asleep holding her.

Haley was in a foul mood. Roger had gotten out of the corral and was nowhere to be found. She'd searched since morning light for the calf and the rooster she knew was bound to be right on his tail.

She had thought that Blackjack was smarter than this. After all, he was in his midlife. It wasn't as if he was a young gun like Roger was.

Roger's mother was still in the corral, looking bored. Lauren and Chase had gone into Tyler for the weekend with the big truck. They were picking up a few new mares. Alex had agreed to watch Ricky down at the diner until her shift ended at two. Haley was supposed to take over watching him for the night; that is if she could find Roger and Blackjack in time.

She was about to give up when she heard the rooster crow behind one of the old hay barns in the south field.

When she rode around the corner, she jumped from her horse and rushed to aid Roger, who was stuck in an old watering hole. His legs and chest were covered in mud as his eyes looked wildly around. When he saw her, he started bawling and thrashing around. Blackjack jumped up on Roger's rear end and stood there looking at her impatiently.

"Well, don't look at me." She stood over the pair, looking down at both of them covered in mud. "I'm not the one who allowed him to walk into that mess."

Shaking her head, she pulled the rope off her saddle and wrapped it around the calf's body. Now she was as muddy as they were and had water in her boots. Tying off the rope to the saddle, she jumped on and started walking Dash back until the little calf was freed.

Roger lay there on the dry ground, breathing hard. When she walked over, he closed his eyes with relief.

"Looks like you two have been at it a while." Squatting down, she patted the calf's neck. "Think you can make it back to the barn?" she asked, knowing she wouldn't get an answer.

It took a few minutes for the calf to catch his breath. When he gained his feet, Blackjack was right there next to him. "Well, come on then." She jumped back on Dash's back, keeping the rope lose around Roger's neck to make sure he didn't wander off again.

"Think you two learned your lesson this time? This is the fourth time this month I've had to search you guys down. If this continues—" She heard thunder in the distance and looked at the sky. From the looks of things, she'd make it back to the house just as the rain started.

"Damn, think you two can pick it up a bit?" she asked. The calf looked up at her, and she could see that he was almost too tired to walk at this pace. She sighed. "Looks like we'll get a little wet then." She frowned and started dreaming about a hot shower and a warm bed next to Wes.

By the time they walked up to the barn, the mud was completely washed from the three of them. Now she had even more water in her boots as she let Roger back into his corral. Blackjack had disappeared near the hen house at the edge of the yard.

By the time she kicked off her boots and walked through the back door, she was frozen.

"What happened to you?" Alex asked. She was standing at the stove, stirring a big pot of macaroni and cheese. Ricky sat at the table, his leg swinging as he colored in his Spiderman coloring book.

"Found Roger." She hung up her jacket and reached down to take off her socks. "He was stuck in the old watering hole behind the south hay barn."

Alex laughed. "That calf is too smart for his own good."

"Maybe this time they'll learn their lesson."

"Was Blackjack with him?" Alex looked over her shoulder at her.

"Of course." She sat down, closed her eyes, and dreamed of a cup of hot chocolate. When she opened them, Alex sat a cup in front of her.

"Hot chocolate?" she asked.

Alex nodded. "I saw you come around the corner of the barn covered in mud and knew you'd want one."

"You are a saint." She grabbed the mug and sipped.

"Why is it raining so much this year?" Alex asked, going back to the stove and removing the pan from the heat.

Haley shrugged. "I'm just glad it's not—"

A loud crash of thunder sounded in the distance. "Damn. Never mind," Haley said, hanging her head.

Ricky started saying damn over and over again as Alex laughed.

"I'm telling," Alex said between laughs.

"I don't suppose I can bribe you?" Haley asked.

Alex shook her head and set a large bowl of mac and cheese in front of her. Just then the back door opened, and Grant walked in, soaking wet.

Alex walked over to him and kissed him. "Taking showers outside again?"

He chuckled. "All the chickens are up. Including that crazy rooster," he said, pulling off his jacket.

"Well, we'll eat dinner here, since Haley took forever getting her calf and rooster back."

Haley looked over at the clock and realized it was a quarter past six. She'd had no clue it had taken her so long to find the wayward animals. Wes was supposed to be back from physical therapy around eight.

"Sorry." She took a bite of the mac and cheese and smiled. "You know, mine doesn't come out this good." She smiled when Ricky dug into his bowl.

Alex sat down next to Grant and smiled. "That's because you don't know the magic ingredient."

"Yeah, yeah." She sighed as she took another bite. "Love. You've told me a million times."

"That's right, Ricky," Alex said as she made sure Ricky's bowl didn't land on the floor. "Auntie Alex makes the best mac and cheese because she loves you more than Haley does." Haley laughed and finished off her bowl before Ricky.

After they finished eating, Grant and Alex helped her clean up then headed back to their place down the street.

She took Ricky upstairs to give him a bath because he was covered in mac and cheese. She desperately wanted a hot shower; she felt like she had mud caked in every pore.

As she watched Ricky play in the bath, she tried not to focus on the growing storm outside. Every now and then lightning would flash and she tried not to jump each time, but Ricky was catching on to her mood.

By the time she pulled him from the cool water and dressed him in his warm PJ's, he looked pretty tired.

She let him play with the trucks as she showered quickly and dressed in an old pair of sweats.

"What do you say you come downstairs with me and watch some cartoons?"

He nodded and held onto her a little more tightly. They walked downstairs and watched cartoons tucked in a large blanket together until a loud bang shook the house and the lights flipped off. She'd turned on the flashlight she had grabbed, but it did little to reassure her.

She didn't want to text Wes because she knew he was driving back from his physical therapy appointment in Dallas. Just then her phone beeped. Looking down, she saw the text come in from Wes.

"Just heard on the radio there's a tornado warning for Anderson County. Better head to the storm shelter."

She froze. This was the first time she'd been alone during one of these. There had been plenty of warning over the years, and each one had taken a toll on her nerves, but usually, her sisters had been there with her.

"Haley?" She received another text just as her phone beeped again. This time it was Lauren asking how she was doing.

A memory flashed in her mind; her mother was carrying her from her bedroom upstairs. She was running and singing to her. Then they were outside, and lightning blinded her as thunder crashed all around them.

She could see the shelter door was open. Her sisters stood at the bottom of the stairs, but then she looked up and saw the dark cyclone and screamed. Her mother jolted. Then Haley was flying through the air until she landed on her sister at the bottom of the shelter.

Another beep sounded. She looked down at the phone. It was Lauren again.

"Are you in the shelter with Ricky?"

Ricky! Haley looked down at the sleeping boy in her arms and something clicked on.

The little boy in her arms depended on her. Wes needed her. They were going to get married and start a family of their own. Her sisters needed her to help with the ranch.

Shoving her phone into her pocket, she grabbed up Ricky, wrapped him in the blanket, and started running from the room. When she opened the back door, the wind and rain hit her face. She felt Ricky stir in her arms, but she covered him with the blanket and cooed to him.

"It's okay. We have to go play down in the shelter for a while," Haley said, tucking him closer to her body. They were halfway across the yard, both dogs right on her heels when she looked up and saw hell heading right for her.

CHAPTER 13

His physical therapist was a moron, he thought as he walked to his car. How is it possible that he hurt more after one hour with the woman than he had after a two-hour emergency surgery?

He was fifteen minutes from Fairplay when he noticed the dark clouds in front of him. Flipping on the news, he listened to the weather. When he heard they were in a warning zone, he pulled over and texted Haley.

When she didn't reply, he tried calling her with the same results.

Tossing his phone down, he did one of the dumbest things he'd ever done in his life. He headed into the eye of the storm to save the woman he loved.

"She's not answering." Lauren paced back and forth in their hotel room. "Why isn't she answering me?" She felt like throwing the phone but held it tighter.

"Maybe the storm has knocked out the cell tower," Chase suggested, his eyes glued to the news on the TV set.

When her phone beeped, she almost dropped it.

"It's Alex, they're in their shelter. She says it's hailing there." Lauren turned to Chase. "Chase."

"I know." He walked over to her and hugged her. "I'll go check out." He rushed from the room.

They were over an hour away, but it would make her feel better to be heading home. She walked over and tossed her clothes into her bag, not caring if she left anything behind.

Five minutes later, they were in the car, heading south, not knowing what they were driving into.

Grant hit the outskirts of town and gasped. The glass in every building downtown was gone. People were standing outside, looking like they were all in shock.

As he drove through the streets of the town, he was glad to see that the bank was still standing, but Mama's and the bookstore were totaled. The front wall of Mama's was completely gone, as well as the roof of the bookstore.

The empty building next door was completely gutted. All that stood were the brick walls on either side.

He stopped and yelled out to Jamella, who was standing there holding a towel over her head. Willard, the cook was sitting next to her holding his arm.

"Are you okay?" He started to get out.

"Lordy, boy. Dat was some shaker. I'm fine. Lookie, here come da big sheriff to save me."

Wes watched with amusement as Sheriff Miller rushed out of his car and grabbed Jamella into a big hug and kissed her square on the lips.

"Don't ever scare me like that again. When I tell you to take shelter, I mean it."

Jamella blushed and patted his shoulder. "Lookie, now everyone knowd about us." She motioned to Wes and Willard.

"I don't give a damn who finds out. It's about time it got out anyway." The sheriff nodded over to him.

Wes would have stayed to help, but he had someone else on his mind. Slamming his door, he tried to text and call Haley one more time. He'd been trying for the seven minutes that it had taken him to get into town.

There was still no reply. He hit the gas and barreled through some debris with his truck. There were tree limbs and trash all over the road, but he knew his truck could handle most of it. When he reached the outskirts of town, the roads cleared up and he thought for a moment that maybe it hadn't hit this far out. Then he turned the corner and saw that a full-sized tree was down, blocking his path to Saddleback. It would take several men and some very large chainsaws to clear the path.

Jumping from his truck, he left the engine running as he climbed over the downed tree. He scraped his arms and legs on the pine branches but didn't feel any pain. When he finally cleared the tree, he rushed towards the iron gates at Saddleback. Half of the letters were missing and some of the fence was twisted.

It was too dark for him to see if the house was still standing so he rushed on until lights hit him. Turning, he saw Alex and Grant drive up in a truck. Alexis' face was masked with concern.

"Have you heard from Haley?" she screamed as she

opened her door and scooted over to allow him in next to her.

"No, you?"

Alex shook her head. "It took us a while to get out of our drive. We had to pull some trees out of the way."

"My truck's stuck behind a downed pine just back at the bend." He nodded, his eyes glued to the house in front of them. It looked intact, but he couldn't see past the first floor.

Before the truck stopped, he jumped out and was running towards the front door yelling her name.

"They'd be in the shelter," Alex called behind him.

He took off running towards the back of the house. "You check in the house. I'll check back there." He turned the corner of the house and gasped. Here the damage was obvious. Half the barn was gone. The roof and hay were strung all over the yard. Horses, cows, and even some goats were walking around the yard looking weather-worn.

He glanced over to the shelter and noticed that the door stood wide open. Calling her name, he rushed over to the door, his heart beating in his ears.

He pulled out his cell phone and flipped on the flashlight app. He heard Ricky start to cry and rushed to the bottom of the stairs. Haley was lying at the bottom, on top of Ricky, who looked up and blinked at the bright light.

"Here," he called over his shoulder. "They're here." He bent down and gently removed Ricky, who clung to him with a death grip.

Since he had to set his flashlight down, it was too dark to see if the boy was injured. He was halfway up the stairway when Grant appeared.

"Is he okay?" he asked, reaching for the boy.

"Don't know. Haley's hurt." He rushed back to the bottom of the stairs. Grant was beside him, holding a flashlight as Alex tried to calm Ricky down at the top of the stairs.

He saw the blood on Haley's forehead and shoulder and gasped. There was a board with nails sticking out of it embedded in her left shoulder.

"Don't remove it," Grant said, rushing back over with a large towel from the cabinet across the room.

He took it and applied pressure to her other cuts. Grant took over, so he could run his hands over her, making sure she didn't have any broken bones. He could see her breathing and felt a steady pulse, but that didn't stop him from worrying.

"Sheriff says an ambulance is on its way. They will have a crew remove the tree," Alex said from the top of the stairs. "Lauren and Chase are half an hour away."

He didn't even acknowledge them; his mind was completely focused on Haley.

"Haley?" he said when she started to move. Holding her steady, he murmured, "Hold still, honey."

Her eyes opened, and she reached out for him. "Ricky?" she said in a weak voice.

"He's here, he's okay. Everyone is okay," he assured her, brushing her dark hair away from her face and taking stock of a few cuts along her forehead.

"I jumped. I couldn't throw him like mama did. I just couldn't let him go. So, I jumped. Oh, my leg," she cried when she started to sit up.

"Shhh," he said. "It's okay. You've broken it. An ambulance is on the way. Hold still until they get here."

"I couldn't throw him. I couldn't," she repeated.

"You did great. You did the right thing," He said, trying not to break.

"Why didn't she jump?" she asked, her green eyes going dark with tears. "Why?" she repeated before fainting.

Wes stood over Haley and waited for her eyes to open again. She'd been in and out of consciousness since they had arrived at the small clinic, which was serving as a triage clinic for now. He still had pressure on her wounds, but his patience was wearing thin. The small room was full of other people, all holding towels up to their cuts, or helping loved ones who were injured. The place was loud and crazy.

His parents had found him a few minutes ago. He'd called them when he'd arrived at the clinic with Haley. They hadn't been affected and been out helping others since the storm had ended.

When the doctor walked back in looking a little frazzled, he got everyone's attention.

"We need those of you who aren't injured to go to the church's gym, across the street. We don't have enough room here to house everyone who isn't injured. Those who have severe injuries or people with small children can have one family member stay with them. But"—he raised his voice over the grumbles— "in order to help everyone, my staff and I need to be able to move around in here."

Wes looked over to his folks and Haley's family and nodded. "I'll let everyone know how she's doing."

Lauren started to object, but Chase tugged on her arm.

"Let's get Ricky home. We need to tend to the animals. Wes will keep us posted."

Once the room was half cleared, the doctor and nurses started moving around.

"Wes." Doctor Conner nodded to him as he stepped up to Haley and looked at the chunk of wood sticking out of her shoulder.

Then there were nurses there, pushing his hands away as they got to work on her. "Why don't you sit down, sweetie. Let us take care of your girl now," one of them said, walking him to a chair a few feet away.

He sat there and watched as they did their magic, cleaning and dressing all her wounds.

"We need to move her, so we can get x-rays on that leg. I think it's a clean break, but I'd like to make sure."

He nodded and stood. "I'd like to go with her, if possible."

The nurse nodded. "Follow me." She started wheeling Haley's bed down the hallway.

Haley reached up for his hand. Her wrist was covered in bandages. He gently took it. He didn't know tears had been falling down his face until she reached up and wiped one away.

Less than an hour later, as he watched the nurse building a cast on Haley's right leg, he called his family and hers and updated them.

The doctor was going to release her and let her go home, with strict instructions that she sees him again in a week. It took another half an hour for the nurse to finish putting on Haley's new red cast.

"In a few weeks, we can give you a removable cast, one that you can take off to shower," she said, handing

Haley some crutches. "Have you ever used crutches before?"

She shook her head and winced a little with pain. As the nurse gave her instructions, Wes talked to the doctor about her other injuries.

"She has seven stitches in her shoulder, a few others here and there. We'll need to see her in a week, once everything settles down around here." He looked around the room, which was still pretty full, with more and more people being brought in all the time.

By the time they drove through town, it was too dark to see anything. Most of the power was out, except for at the clinic, the church across the way, and the town hall on the corner.

They could see a large crowd gathered at the town hall. Other car lights and floodlights were at several houses along the roads as people searched for others.

"Wes," Haley said, touching his arm. "Maybe we should stop and help?"

He nodded. "But you will stay in the truck. Got it?" When she nodded, he parked and hopped out.

Wes walked up to where the sheriff was addressing everyone and stood next to Grant and Chase.

"Hey," he said.

"Hey." Chase looked over at the truck. "How's she doing?"

"Good."

"If you want, take her back to Saddleback, then come back. We're going to go house by house to make sure everyone is okay. Lauren, Alex, and Ricky are there. I've got the generator going out there, so there is power."

Wes nodded. "I'll be back."

By the time he persuaded Haley to stay with her sisters, they were already driving up the long drive. All the lights were on in the main floor and when they drove up, Lauren and Alex were on the front porch, ready to help Haley in.

"The guys called," Lauren said, holding up a cooler. "There's water and sandwiches. Enough for a dozen people. I'll make some more and bring them down later."

He shook his head. "The roads aren't safe. There are several power lines down. The crews are working on it now. Just give us a call and I'll come back for them." She nodded. "Take care of her," he said when Haley and Alex were inside. "Here." He handed her Haley's pills and the instructions from the clinic.

When he drove back into town, there were more floodlights from the construction crews. Hundreds of people worked in the lit-up areas, searching for survivors of some of the worst-hit homes.

An hour later, dog rescue teams arrived, followed by a flood of people from the Red Cross and other charity organizations.

By morning, there were three large medical tents set up in the parking lot of the town hall. They had set up a kitchen at the church, where everyone could walk in and get fresh water, food, or rest if needed.

The high school housed the families who had been displaced, and donation trucks flooded the parking lot. Volunteers had cleaned most of the roads, so travel in and out of town was a lot smoother.

Power had been restored to most of the areas that had sustained minor damage. The gas and water for the entire town was still down. They'd been told that it might take up to a month before the gas could be turned back on, though less than that for the water.

So far, Wes had heard of two casualties. He'd helped dig out a few survivors himself but was thankful he hadn't known any of those who had lost their lives.

By the next evening, when he, Chase, and Grant returned to Saddleback, they were all exhausted, dirty, and starved.

$\mathcal{H}$aley watched her sisters come in from her spot on the couch. She'd been babied ever since arriving home late last night. She'd slept through most of the night but woke early with pain in her shoulder and leg.

Alex had cooked her favorite breakfast. She followed it up by swallowing a half dozen pills that were large enough to feed to her horses.

Then Ricky settled down on her lap, so they could watch Bug's Bunny while her sisters went out to try and catch the loose animals.

When they came back in around lunchtime, they were both caked in mud.

"That calf of yours is either the smartest animal I've ever seen or the dumbest," Lauren said, shaking her head.

"What has Roger done now?" she asked, laughing.

"You don't want to know," Alex said, stepping in beside her sister. Lauren had a lot of mud on her, but Alex was completely covered. Haley could even see some coming out of her sister's ears.

"I don't know how you catch that little bugger," Alex said, trying to wipe her face with a large towel.

Lauren laughed. "You should have seen it. I think when it comes to roping a calf, your sister is out of practice."

"I am not!" Alex gasped, then shook her finger at Haley. "That is no ordinary calf. He's like a . . . a supervillain." She put her hands on her hips.

Haley smiled; her sisters were the best medicine in the world.

By that afternoon, when the men walked into the house as dirty as their wives had been, all the animals were accounted for and safe. Old Betty had been the only casualty, but since the blue truck hadn't run in the last three months, everyone considered it an acceptable loss. Lauren told her that the barn would have to be repaired and that they had lost half of their hay reserves for the winter.

When Wes walked into the room, she smiled and tried not to let it show that she'd missed her pain pill for lunch. She didn't want to take it since it made her sleepy.

He walked over to her, placed a kiss on her cheek, and frowned down at her. "You're in pain," he said, sitting next to her.

She shook her head. "I'll be fine. How bad is it?"

He leaned his head back and sighed. "Mama's, the bookstore, a dozen or so houses along first and third."

"Any deaths?" she asked quietly since Ricky was napping on the couch across from her.

He nodded and held up three fingers. "Several animals as well. There are a dozen dogs running through town. The shelter is trying to pick up all of them and hold them until the owners can pick them up."

"Anyone we know?" she asked.

He nodded. "Steve, from the bank, lost his father. He survived the tornado but died from a stroke while helping dig his neighbor out of the rubble. The other two I didn't know." He shrugged. "If it's okay, I'm going to go shower. Would you like to stay here?"

She nodded, knowing that the slightest movement caused the pain to triple. He stood up, then leaned over her and kissed her slowly. "I'll be back soon. I love you."

She smiled then shook her head. "Get some rest. You look beat. I'll still be here in the morning."

He nodded. "But tomorrow, you're coming home with me for good." He smiled. "I don't want more than one night without you by my side."

She nodded, not knowing what to say. Her throat had closed up with want.

"Wes," Alex said, rushing into the room. "Oh, good you're still here." She shoved a large container into his hands. "Dinner. Steak, potatoes, carrots, and rolls. Just nuke it for five minutes when you get home."

Wes nodded, then walked out of the room.

"When are you going to put him out of his misery?" Alex asked, walking over and sitting next to her.

"What do you mean?"

"That boy loves you; he's proven to you that he's back to stay."

"I know," she nodded. "We are engaged." She held up her ring finger.

Her sister just looked at her, then finally said, "You

know what I mean. I bet you haven't told him you love him, again."

Haley frowned. Just then she realized that her sister was right. Since he'd returned, she hadn't said those words to him. He'd told her several times that he loved her.

Could that be what was missing? Could that be the reason she felt like there was a rift between them still?

She sat there for the next hour and thought about it. Wes had done everything since returning home to prove to her that he'd made a mistake. He'd apologized, proven to her he was reliable and had even won her heart back. Yet, she'd held back something as important as saying those words to him.

Could that be the only thing she'd been missing? It couldn't be that simple, could it?

Chase walked in an hour later, freshly showered, with a big bowl of popcorn in one hand. "Want to watch an old flick?"

She shook her head. "No, thank you. I need your help." She laughed. "I might need everyone's help." She looked down at her cast.

Wes woke the next morning sorer than he'd ever been. Every muscle in his body ached. The hot shower did little to soothe the aches and pains, so he stayed in there an extra ten minutes until he felt almost human again. When he walked into his living room to head over to the main house, he was shocked to see Chase sitting on his couch, looking pissed.

"What's up?" He sat across from him.

"Grant needs our help down at the courthouse. It seems that old man Peterson is trying to sue us."

"What?" Wes stood up. "The man we pulled from the pile of rubble last night? That used to be his house?"

Chase nodded. "He's down at the courthouse and wants to meet with us all in"—Chase looked at his watch — "ten minutes ago."

"Damn, well come on then. Let's go nip this in the bud." Wes walked to the door.

Chase drove and Wes hardly noticed that most of the town had been cleaned up. He did notice that there were large boards covering the front of the bookstore and Mama's place. He'd had a long talk with Jamella the day before; she was on board to rebuild and had even talked about taking over the building next door to expand. The bookstore owner, Holly Bridles, had also explained to everyone that she would rebuild.

Now as they parked in front of the courthouse, he started to worry. Not only was Grant standing in front of the town hall, but almost everyone in town stood out there as well.

The sun was shining and if he hadn't known better, he would have never guessed that a large tornado had hit there just two days ago.

"What's all this? Is old man Peterson going to sue the whole town of Fairplay?"

Chase chuckled. "No, but the whole town of Fairplay came out today to see you get married."

Wes's eyes were glued to the crowd as it parted. Haley stood with the help of her crutches, dressed in a simple cream-colored sundress. Her cuts and bruises went unnoticed as he played over Chase's words in his mind.

"Today?" he asked, without taking his eyes off of Haley.

"If you ever get out of my truck, that is." Chase laughed and got out himself.

Wes followed slowly, not blinking from the sight of the sun streaming through Haley's hair. It felt like it took an eternity for him to walk the pathway towards her. The crowd of people filed in beside the walkway and stood smiling at him.

"Hi," he said, coming to a stop in front of her.

"Hi." She smiled. "Want to get married today?"

He laughed. "I thought you wanted a big wedding?"

Her eyebrows shot up. "How much bigger do you think we could get?" She motioned with her hand to the two hundred guests standing around them in front of the town hall.

He laughed. "I guess you're right." He reached over and took her hand. "I'd love to marry you today."

"Well, that's good," the new mayor, William Davis, said. "Shall we begin?"

"'Bout damn time," someone shouted, followed by a large boom of laughter from the crowd.

After the quick ceremony on the green lawn of the town hall, everyone filed into the First Baptist Church's gym for a reception. Barbeque sandwiches, fried catfish, and baked beans were dished out, followed by watermelon and homemade ice cream.

Someone had given Haley a wheelchair to use so she could wheel herself around and talk to everyone. He took great care in making sure she stayed off her feet, so he ended up wheeling her around most of the day. Her sisters occasionally took over when he was busy talking to someone.

They talked to Sheriff Miller, who was very vocal about his relationship with Jamella. Apparently, the two had been an item for almost ten years without anyone in the town, or her kids, knowing. Wes thought that the two of them were great together.

"They fit, don't they?" Haley smiled and nodded towards the pair.

He chuckled. "I was just thinking the same thing. It's hard to believe that no one guessed about their relationship sooner."

Haley shook her head. "Alex has been the closest to Jamella for years. You would have thought that she had some clue. But look at her." She chuckled. "She's still in complete and utter shock."

He looked at his new sister-in-law and laughed. "She looks like she just found out that the world is round."

They both laughed.

"I hear she's going to take over the empty building next door and build a whole new diner."

He nodded. "She said, and I quote, 'Good ting my insurance is paid up.'" He laughed.

"It's just a good thing she and Willard weren't hurt. It's hard to believe they were in there when the tornado hit."

He nodded and felt even luckier than before. "Really, the whole town was lucky. It could have been so much worse."

Wes hadn't realized how much time had passed since he'd been so entertained, but when someone mentioned that the sun was going down, he realized it was time to head home.

"Shall we get out of here?" he whispered to Haley.

"I thought you'd never ask." She smiled. "I have another surprise for you, but it will have to wait until this is gone." She nodded to her cast.

He shook his head and helped her to stand. "I have everything I could ever want right here." He wrapped his arms around her then dipped his head and kissed her.

When they heard cheering, they both laughed.

She looked up into his eyes, and her green eyes went soft. She'd never looked more beautiful than she did just then.

"I love you, Wes Tanner. I have loved you since the second grade. You're my best friend, my only lover, and the man I want to start a family with."

Tears slid down his face. "Damn," he whispered. "Now you've gone and made me cry in front of the whole town."

She laughed and kissed him again.

"I love you, too. Let's get out of here, so I can show you how much," he whispered in her ear.

*H*aley stood on the hill and looked off towards their house. There were animals roaming the hills, grazing. Four horses—two were hers, two Wes had purchased—two Shetland ponies, three miniature donkeys that she'd rescued after the tornado, three llamas they'd purchased in Tyler, not to mention the three dogs that were running around causing chaos. Wes had built a chicken coop on the side of the barn where Blackjack and several of his harem were housed. In the large pen next to them was Roger, full grown and loving his new home.

She turned in time to watch her husband of four months walking towards her. His new patrol uniform looked damn sexy on him. He'd been on the job for three months and was even taking classes to become a full-blown sheriff. His limp was still present, but he'd fully recovered from his surgery and was growing stronger every day.

She looked down at her leg and smiled. So was she. She'd sworn she'd do everything in her power to never have to wear a cast again. Not only had it made walking, riding, and sex virtually impossible, it had itched like crazy.

"How's my beautiful wife today?" Wes walked up to her and kissed her softly.

"Wonderful. How was work?" She wrapped her arms around his shoulders, enjoying the feel of him.

"Smooth. I guess being an officer of the law in a small town has its perks."

"Oh?"

He smiled. "Mrs. Kennedy baked us one of her world-class blackberry pies."

"Yum." She smiled. "I think she's trying to steal my handsome husband away from me. That's the third pie she's given you this month."

He laughed. "Well, when you have as many grandchildren as she does, I'll allow you to flirt with young men in uniform too." He smiled and pulled her closer.

"Speaking of children." She pulled away and smiled. "How would you like to have one in oh . . . say seven or eight months?"

She saw his eyes go dark, then his smile got huge. "Really?"

She nodded. "Just found out today."

"Woohoo!" He spun her around.

"Of course, now we're in a race with my sisters." She smiled when he sat her back on her feet. "Lauren is due in July, Alex in September, and we're due in November."

"That's a baby every other month," he said, as she laughed. "Just watch, we'll have the best-looking kid around."

She laughed. "Or twins."

PROLOGUE

Reece wiped the blood from his nose and yanked his chin up so his pa wouldn't see that the blow had damaged his soul. When his brother, Ryan, moved to help him up from the dirt, he shook his head to stop him.

"You like hitting little kids, old man?" He stood up and dusted off his Levi's like he had all the time in the world.

"Little brats who don't listen to me deserve to have their asses kicked." His old man stood almost a foot taller than Reece's thirteen-year-old frame. He couldn't wait for the day when he would be taller than the old man, because he knew that was the day he'd walk away and never look back.

"Pa, it was my fault." Ryan started to cover for him. Even though the boys were identical in looks, they were complete opposites in personality.

"I'm the one who didn't shut the gate after Pa asked," Reece said, squinting his eyes at his twin. "I'll go hunt down the horses."

His father grunted and threw him the reins to Buck, his

stallion. "Be back by supper time or you won't get any slop." Reece watched his father walk away without a backward glance.

"Hang on a few minutes, and I'll saddle up Star," Ryan said before rushing towards the barn.

"No," Reece called out. "Star will just slow me down. I can get the damn horses myself." He jumped on the back of Buck and hightailed it out of the yard.

The dry heat of the day turned to a cool breeze as he flew across the yellow fields. He knew where the three horses would go first, the stream, so he headed towards it with a smile on his face.

This is what he lived for, a moment to himself as he rode across the fields. No old man slapping at you, no brother sticking up for you. Just him and a horse. He leaned down and patted Buck on the neck. "You like to run, don't you?" He smiled when the horse nodded his head. He had a way with animals; they always seemed to listen and never gave him shit back.

It took him almost two hours to get to the stream, and by the time he gathered the three horses and tied their leads together, he was covered in sweat and dirt. Tying the rope to a tree, he pulled off his soiled clothes and jumped in the cool water for a swim.

After ten minutes in the cool water, he calculated that he wouldn't get home until an hour after dark. Damn. He was hungry.

Pulling his dirty clothes on, he jumped on Buck's back and yanked the other horses to follow him. When he finally rode up, the back-porch light was the only one on in the small house. It had taken him too long to get back, mostly because he hadn't wanted to injure a horse by rushing in the dark.

There wasn't a warm plate in the oven waiting for him, no sweet note from a mother telling him to eat something —nothing. Except for an empty feeling as he climbed the dark stairs with achy muscles and a sore backside from the long ride.

When Reece sat down on his bed, Ryan sat up and flipped on the small light.

"I saved you a sandwich." He nodded to a plate sitting on the box he used as a nightstand.

"Thanks."

"Were they at the stream?"

"Yeah," he said in between bites.

"Damn, I'm sorry, man."

Reece shrugged his shoulders. "My fault."

"Man, I can't wait till the day we can get out of here." Ryan lay back down and stared up at the ceiling.

It was a common conversation of theirs. They'd been planning their escape since a month after their mother had passed of cancer shortly after their tenth birthday. That's when their dad had turned mean.

"Yeah, until then, I guess I need to make sure I close the gate."

Ryan chuckled. "Did you enjoy the ride, at least?"

Reece nodded. "Best moment of the month so far." He smiled at his brother and flipped off the light. The two boys lay on their beds, identical dreams of escaping in their heads as they drifted off.

CHAPTER 1

Melissa walked into the empty clinic and smiled. The small waiting room was quiet, but she knew that within the hour, it would be full of crying kids and worrying mamas. She'd never imagined herself back in her hometown, taking over the clinic that everyone in town had been in at some moment in their lives.

"Well?" her older brother said from behind her. "What do you think?" Grant wrapped his arm around her shoulders and smiled down at her.

She smiled up at him, wanting to squeal with joy. "Thanks for buying me breakfast." She nodded to the coffee in her hand. He'd taken her to Mama's, the best— and only—diner in town. It had just been remodeled and was busier than ever.

Melissa was staying with Grant, his wife, Alex, and their daughter, Laura, out at their new ranch just outside of town. At least until she could find a place of her own.

There were a few possibilities, but she had yet to make up her mind about which one to move in to.

It had been almost two weeks since she'd returned to town and had bumped into Dr. Conner, who had quickly informed her that he was looking to hire a new head nurse for the clinic. Bonnie, the head nurse who had worked at the clinic for as long as anyone could remember, had retired earlier that year. Dr. Conner had told her that he was desperate to hire someone who could put things in order again around the clinic. He was about ten years older than Melissa and had been working at the clinic since moving into town almost six years ago. Melissa had noted that he wasn't a bad looking man; he was tall, had jet-black hair and dark eyes, something she'd always found very attractive in a man. She'd worked with plenty of doctors in Houston where she'd gone to school and done her internship, but she had immediately wondered about working with Dr. Conner since it was a small town and people talked.

She'd run into him at the grocery store, and he'd almost begged her to at least stop by and look into the clinic. She'd put it off for a while, but after applying for a few jobs in the city, she'd decided that sticking around her hometown for a while couldn't hurt.

When she had stopped by, all the other employees had been so accepting and kind, and when Dr. Conner had presented her with an offer, she'd jumped at it.

Now as she looked around the room, she couldn't help but smile.

"Anytime, little sis." He leaned down and placed a kiss on her cheek. "Anytime. Well, I'd better get back to the house. I bet my girls are up already."

She smiled, remembering how cute her niece was. Her soft blonde hair, chubby baby cheeks, and eyes matched Grant's perfectly.

"Go be a husband and daddy." She reached up and kissed his cheek. He had changed so much in the past few years that she still had a hard time believing he was the same man. Gone were the chubby cheeks, the thick glasses, and the insecurity. Now her brother looked more like a movie star than the awkward boy she'd been raised looking up to, which only made her look up to him even more.

By the time she'd flipped on all the lights in the clinic, several of the staff had arrived and were preparing for the day. Since Fairplay was a small town, she already knew everyone who worked there. When the doctor walked in at a quarter past eight, the waiting room and the three small examining rooms were already full. Apparently, it was early flu season and most of the kids in grade school had passed it to one another.

By the end of her first day, she was exhausted and yet strangely full of energy. She knew there was a lot she could improve on at the small clinic and hoped that everyone else would be as excited as she was to make things flow more efficiently. During her lunch, she had written up a small list of items she would fix first.

After the doors were closed and locked for the day, she knocked on Dr. Conner's office door.

"Come in." She took a deep breath hand opened the door.

"Oh, Melissa," he said, setting down a folder. He waved her in and motioned to the chair. "So, how was your first day?"

"Great." She smiled, feeling a little nervous.

"I can't thank you enough for helping us out. So, what did you think?" He folded his arms on the desk and waited.

She took a deep breath. "I have a few suggestions." She looked down at the paper in her hands.

"Great." He held out his hand for the paper.

She waited as he read through her list, her fingers folded in her lap, and her eyes focused on his face, waiting for any emotions.

"These could all work out very well." He smiled and looked up at her. "Some of them might take some time for us to adjust to, but I think we can all make an effort. When would you like to start on these?"

Her eyebrows shot up. There was no arguing, no complaining, no power pushing. She wasn't used to it. At the hospital she had interned at in Houston, she'd been laughed at when she'd made a small suggestion and had been told to just follow the rules that someone much smarter than she had come up with years and years ago.

"I can come in early tomorrow and start on the organizational parts. I can write up the changes to help the other employees."

"Wonderful." He stood and handed the paper back to her. "I knew you were going to be good for us."

She smiled and took the paper from him. For the first time since entering the medical field, she felt like someone had listened to her opinions.

When she left the clinic, Alex was sitting in her truck waiting for her. She honked the horn and waved her over.

"So, how was your first day?" she asked.

"Crazy." Melissa smiled as she got into the truck.

"Busy. And the most wonderful day I've had in years."
She smiled.

Alex laughed. "You belong here, sister," she said as she pulled out onto Main Street.

They chatted as Alex drove slowly through the small town. Much had changed since Melissa had left almost six years ago. The tornado that had ripped through town a little over a year ago had damaged most of the buildings in the older part of town. Now most of them had new storefronts and a fresh coat of paint. New streetlights and park benches lined the newly paved roads. The playground at the city park was bigger than ever.

The mayor, William Davis, a longtime Fairplay resident, had used the FEMA money well. Even the old movie theater was up and running now.

"I can't believe how much the town has grown."

Alex laughed. "Really?" She shrugged her shoulders. "I guess since I have never left, I can't see it, other than all the fixes after the tornado."

"It must have been hard when it hit."

Alex nodded. "We had some scary times, but everything turned out alright."

"Haley was hurt, wasn't she?" Haley and Melissa had been friends as kids and had spent the night at one another's houses at least once a month.

"Yeah, she broke her leg. She was banged up pretty good."

"I haven't gone out to see their new place yet." Melissa frowned and looked at her hands. "I guess I've been focusing on myself since getting into town."

"Don't worry about it. She has her hands full with those twins of theirs."

Melissa smiled, thinking of Haley and Wes's two boys. She'd bumped into Haley at the Grocery Stop and had cooed over the chubby boys. "They are so cute. I'll have to swing by their place and smother them with kisses again."

Alex laughed. "I can't believe she's the one that had twins. They run in the family, you know."

"Really?"

"Yeah, our grandfather was a twin, and we have twin cousins." She glanced over at her. "I think you met one of them at our wedding. Reece?"

"Hmm, I don't remember."

"He's tall, dark hair, green eyes, and had a sour look on his face the entire time." Alex smiled. "He's the younger one. Both boys had it hard growing up." She shook her head. "My aunt died young and their father was an ass. No one has heard from his brother, Ryan, in years." She shook her head and frowned.

"It must have been hard on them, losing their mother so young. I know Haley always talked about losing your mother. Then your dad died when we were fourteen and her grief started all over." She remembered that day. Haley had stopped spending the night at her house after that, and she had pulled away from their friendship. She'd always thought it was something she'd done or said to ruin the friendship. In the end, she'd become closer to her friend Holly, who now owned the local bookstore.

"Yeah, it hit her the hardest." Alex shook her head. "She was a daddy's girl. She was the only one of us that couldn't really remember our mother."

They drove through the gates of Grant and Alex's place, and Melissa looked at their lovely home. It sat down in a little valley. The large stone house sat off to the left and there was a big gray barn to the right. Her brother had so many animals, she had a hard time keeping up.

"What?" Alex asked when Melissa laughed.

"It's just that my brother has so many animals." She giggled again.

"What's so funny about that?"

"We never had any growing up. He knew how to ride, we both did, but now he owns horses, cows, chickens, and…" She giggled again. "Goats. I mean, he spoils those goats more than he does anything else."

"Tell me about it." Alex rolled her eyes and smiled. "They can do no wrong. Do you know that he's thinking of building a new barn, just for the goats?"

She nodded. "He told me over breakfast."

Alex grunted. "That man has a soft spot for those damn goats." She stopped the truck and turned to her with a smile on her face. "But, then again, so do I. Buttercup saved my life once, you know."

Melissa laughed. She'd heard the story of how the little goat had helped when Alex had been knocked out by Mrs. Nolan, the ex-mayor's wife.

"And Junior saved your brother." She nodded towards the large dog that hobbled across the yard to greet them.

The dog's thick dark fur hid the scars that everyone knew were there. Most of his left hind leg was so badly damaged, he spent most of his time lying down. Alex and Grant doted on the dog more than any other animal on their small farm.

"For that, we all owe him everything." Melissa knelt and rubbed the dog's thick fur as his tail thumped in the dirt. She got teary every time she thought about the scare they'd had after Mrs. Nolan had shot her brother point-blank. She'd spent almost a month at her parents' place until her brother had gotten back on his feet. The little dog had gotten the worst of it, though. And Mrs. Nolan was rotting away at some state-run loony bin in Rusk, Texas.

When she looked up, she saw her brother standing on the porch holding little Laura, as she liked to call her. They had named their daughter after Alex's mother, who had died in a tornado that hit Fairplay when the girls were very young.

She watched as Alex walked up and hugged and kissed her family. Something inside Melissa shifted and for the first time in her adult life, she wished for a moment just like that.

Lauren had given Reece the largest ranch house on the property. It had been sitting empty since they'd put in a few trailers closer to the barns. They had over a dozen men working for them now and, by the looks of it, they needed another dozen.

He'd spent the first day there helping with the cattle and had noticed a beautiful palomino running wild in one of the corrals. When he'd approached it, the beast's ears had perked up. Chase told him that the horse was still untrained and in dire need of breaking.

Chase hadn't had enough time to start working on the horse, and Reece had quickly requested the job.

"You can start on him first thing in the morning," Chase said, patting his back. "Just don't come running to me when the beast kills you. He's an ornery son of a gun."

He'd spent the rest of the day helping the hands brand

the cattle and getting the little ones up to date on shots. It had been a sweaty job, but he'd loved every minute.

When he got back to his place, he realized that the kitchen cupboards were completely empty, and he grabbed his truck keys to head down to the grocery store.

As he drove through the small town, he realized how much he felt at home here. They had visited often when they were kids. Up until their early teens, they had spent a few weeks here every summer to help out. He and his brother had made their best childhood memories here.

Pulling in front of the Grocery Stop, the only grocery store in town, he wondered how long he would stick around. He walked through the aisles, tossing items into his cart and thinking about breaking horses for a living. He'd always dreamed of being able to do that.

Maybe Fairplay was the place to do it. Why not? He knew a lot of people in town and, more important, they knew him. That was key for running a business like this. If they trusted him to do the job, he'd get more work. And there was bound to be a lot of work in these parts. They were less than an hour from Tyler, and there were plenty of smaller towns around that he could drum up business in.

"Well, well," he heard someone purr from behind him. "If it isn't one of the West boys."

He turned to see a busty blonde swaying down the aisle towards him. The tight shorts she wore barely covered her curves, and she was almost busting out of the shirt buttons. It took a few moments for his eyes to wander higher to see the well-groomed face that matched the perfect body.

He'd known Savannah Douglas most of her life. She'd been one of Lauren's best friends when they were younger, but after middle school, he'd seen less and less of her around the farm. She'd grown up in the lap of luxury ever since her folks had hit it big with oil money.

Now she wore the best clothes, drove the most expensive car in town, and was always after something she couldn't get.

He knew that Savannah was the cause of a lot of problems with his cousins over the last few years, but as she walked towards him, everything but the throbbing in his pants left his mind.

"Well, hello. This can't be little Savannah?" he said as she stopped right next to him.

"Which one are you?" She ran a manicured finger up his arm playfully.

"Reece." He smiled down at her.

"Oh, I could never tell you and your brother apart." She leaned closer to him. "I didn't know you were in town. How long are you here for?"

He could smell her perfume and the feel of her breasts pushed up against his chest was sending all his blood away from his head.

"Not sure. I'm thinking of staying on."

"For good?" She gasped a little. He could tell it was all an act, and if his mind had been working, he would have realized he shouldn't be leading her on. But it had been a while since he'd gotten any attention from someone so attractive.

"Maybe."

"Well, I'll simply have to bake you one of my famous pies and bring it over to you. Where are you staying?"

"At the ranch house at the end of the road at Lauren's place."

"Oh." She frowned a little.

"Problem?"

"No." Her smile came back. "Well, I'm sure we'll bump into each other again," she said, taking a step back when a young mother and her kids tried to get by them in the aisle. Savannah stared after the woman and kids. "I simply must be going." She leaned closer and whispered, "I'm looking forward to seeing you." Her eyes traveled up and down him and then rested on his crotch. If he were a teenager, he would have blushed bright red.

He watched her hips as she swayed back down the aisle and out the front door without buying anything.

"That girl is trouble," someone said from behind him.

When he turned around, he saw a very petite redheaded woman standing next to his cart, a full basket of groceries in her hands.

"Holly Bridles. We met at Alex and Grant's wedding and again at Haley and Wes'." She shifted her basket and held out a hand.

He smiled and took it. "I remember. You own a shop…" He tried to remember.

"Bookstore. It's just across the street."

"Right," he nodded, remembering.

"Savannah will toy with you. Besides, she's not allowed on Saddleback Ranch property anymore."

"Oh?" He must have looked surprised because Holly laughed.

"Long story. Ask your cousin one day if you have a few hours to listen to it. So did I hear you right? You're back to stay?"

"Maybe." He took her basket and set it inside his cart. The thing looked heavier than she did, and he could see she was struggling with it. "Why didn't you get a cart?"

"Oh, well, you know how it is. You run inside for one thing and…" She shrugged her shoulders. "You walk out with a cart full." She smiled.

They walked up to the checkout, and he put her basket up for her. They chatted for a while with the checker and when she had her two full bags in her arms, she turned back around to him. "Remember what I said about staying away from Savannah."

He nodded. "Thanks. I'll see you around."

She nodded and then turned and walked out.

"She's right, you know," the woman behind the counter said as she began scanning his items. "Everyone in town knows to steer clear of that girl."

He chuckled. "I think I'm getting the hint," he said, handing over his credit card. Until he could get the full story, Savannah Douglas was on his do-not-touch list.

This is a work of fiction. Names, characters, places, and incidents are either the product of the author's imagination or are used fictitiously, and any resemblance to actual persons, living or dead, business establishments, events, or locales is entirely coincidental.

HOLDING HALEY

DIGITAL ISBN: 978-1-942896-48-7

PRINT ISBN: 978-1-942896-49-4

Copyright © 2014 Jill Sanders

All rights reserved.

Copyeditor: Erica Ellis – inkdeepediting.com

No part of this book may be reproduced, scanned, or distributed in any printed or electronic form without permission. Please do not participate in or encourage piracy of copyrighted materials in violation of the author's rights. Purchase only authorized editions.

ALSO BY JILL SANDERS

The Pride Series

Finding Pride

Discovering Pride

Returning Pride

Lasting Pride

Serving Pride

Red Hot Christmas

My Sweet Valentine

Return To Me

Rescue Me

The Secret Series

Secret Seduction

Secret Pleasure

Secret Guardian

Secret Passions

Secret Identity

Secret Sauce

The West Series

Loving Lauren

Taming Alex

Holding Haley

Missy's Moment

Breaking Travis

Roping Ryan

Wild Bride

Corey's Catch

Tessa's Turn

The Grayton Series

Last Resort

Someday Beach

Rip Current

In Too Deep

Swept Away

High Tide

Lucky Series

Unlucky In Love

Sweet Resolve

Best of Luck

A Little Luck

Silver Cove Series

Silver Lining

French Kiss

Happy Accident

Hidden Charm

A Silver Cove Christmas

Entangled Series – Paranormal Romance

The Awakening

The Beckoning

The Ascension

Haven, Montana Series

Closer to You

Never Let Go

Holding On

Pride Oregon Series

A Dash of Love

My Kind of Love

Season of Love

Tis the Season

Dare to Love

Where I Belong

Wildflowers Series

Summer Nights

Summer Heat

Stand Alone Books

Twisted Rock

For a complete list of books:

http://JillSanders.com

Jill Sanders is a New York Times, USA Today, and international bestselling author of Sweet Contemporary Romance, Romantic Suspense, Western Romance, and Para-normal Romance novels. With over 55 books in eleven series, translations into several different languages, and audio-books there's plenty to choose from. Look for Jill's bestselling stories wherever romance books are sold or visit her at jillsanders.com

Jill comes from a large family with six siblings, including an identical twin. She was raised in the Pacific Northwest and later relocated to Colorado for college and a successful IT career before discovering her talent for writing sweet and sexy page-turners. After Colorado, she decided to move south, living in Texas and now making her home along the Emerald Coast of Florida. You will find that the settings of several of her series are inspired by her time spent living in these areas. She has two sons and off-set the testosterone in her house by adopting three furry little ladies that provide her company while she's locked in her writing cave. She enjoys heading to the beach, hiking, swimming, wine-tasting, and pickleball with her husband, and of course writing. If you have read any of her books, you may also notice that there is a love of food, especially sweets! She has been blamed for a few added pounds by her assistant, editor, and fans… donuts or pie anyone?

facebook.com/JillSandersBooks

twitter.com/JillMSanders

bookbub.com/authors/jill-sanders